Twisted Souls

Reapers of Havoc MC

Ashlee M. Edmonds

Cover Design by EmCat Designs

Editing by Fox Proofs Editing

Proofreading by Geeky Good Edits

CONTENTS

This book is dedicated to the Wild Ones.
The free spirits with a gypsy soul.
The ones who crave more out of life,
Constantly searching for their next adventure.
Keep that fire burning in your soul.

Twisted Souls is book one in the Reapers of Havoc MC series and must be read in order. This series contains darker themes such as dub-con, violence, kidnapping, murder and torture. Please be aware of your triggers before stepping into this world.

Chapter One

ANGEL

Ladies and gentlemen welcome to the shit show. My name is Angel Somers, and I'll be your host on this episode of *How to Be a Stalker*. You'll be following me today as I stake out the Reapers of Havoc's clubhouse.

If things go as planned, we'll finally be able to locate the three assholes that I call my best friends. Who, by the way, have mysteriously disappeared. If not, we shall return for another episode tomorrow.

Man, the shit I come up with when I'm bored is wild.

Is this seriously what my life is turning into? A reality TV show? Ew, I hate those.

I'm actually not a stalker. Calm down. Hear me out for a minute before you jump to conclusions.

I'd like to think of it as being a really good friend. You know, the kind of friend who sits outside all the places you might possibly be with the hopes of seeing any sight of you.

Okay, fine. Maybe I'm being a little stalker-ish, but it's definitely for a good reason. So, you can stop judging me now. Gimme a chance to explain and you'll see that my reasons are valid.

You see, it's been a whole freaking week since the guys ghosted me, and I'm going a little mad. Not like *mad*, mad. More like Mad Hatter mad.

Well, maybe a little bit of both, but that's beside the point.

It's been a week since I've seen or heard from them. They dropped me off at home and then pulled a Houdini on my ass.

See, I told you I had a good reason. I'm sure all stalkers probably say that, but— whatevs.

The guys and I never went more than a day without seeing or speaking to each other. Hence why I'm here, staking out the clubhouse and looking for the assholes.

I'll most likely forgive their shitty behavior, but only after hearing whatever lame-ass excuse they conjure up in their tiny, little man brains that made them think this would be okay. Oh, and it better be good too. Otherwise, I'll be kicking their asses to the moon and back.

Never in a million years would I believe they'd do this to me. Clearly, I was wrong.

Leaving me alone for this long is entirely out of character for them. In my nineteen years of life, I've spent fifteen of them with the guys by my side. Something is off. I can feel it in my bones. I just haven't been able to figure out what, yet.

Staring at the entrance to the clubhouse, I'm watching the Reapers come and go. Just carrying on with their lives as usual.

I've been wishing upon a star that I could catch King as he arrives. Hoping that he would give me some information on the guys' whereabouts. Apparently, the stars are conspiring against me lately because I haven't seen him all week.

The rest of these fools are acting as if three of their club members haven't just up and disappeared. Plus, they're ignoring the fact that I've been casing the joint for an entire week. Which is just plain rude.

I know you see my psycho ass sitting here.

I'm purposely flipping each one of them the bird when they look my way.

These old ass bikers are playing dumb even though they know exactly who I am, and what

I'm doing here. I can almost guarantee they know where the hell my guys are too. I'm getting impatient sitting around waiting for King or one of the guys to show up.

I've been sitting on my Ducati since early this morning casing the joint. I'm hangry, irritated, and my ass went numb over an hour ago.

Where the hell are they?

I swear, if I didn't care for them as much as I do, I would block their asses and try to forget they ever existed. I'd just move on with my life and make them suffer the consequences of their actions.

Ha. Hey, a girl can dream, right?

I've run through every scenario possible, and my brain can't begin to fathom a reason good enough for them to leave me like this. Hell, it would take the apocalypse to keep me from them, and I always thought it was the same way for them.

Growing up, it was always the five of us, Royal James, Lucky Newman, Jaxon Rivers, Dante Garcia, and myself. Just us against the world. Ride or fucking die.

Outsiders would try to weasel their way into the group, but no one ever clicked or quite understood the dynamics of our gang.

Lucky and I have been best friends practically since birth. Our moms are lifelong best friends and ended up getting pregnant at the same time. When we got older and started grade school, Lucky became friends with the others. We're all the same age and were in the same grade. Much to their dismay, I would always tag along with them.

While most girls my age were into princesses, Barbies, and My Little Pony, I was into getting dirty, climbing trees, and playing sports.

At first, Royal, Jaxon, and Dante hated playing with a girl. You know, cooties and all that. But, eventually, they warmed up to me.

It was probably around the time I kicked Jacob Grossman in the balls for trying to bully Lucky on the playground. Nobody messes with my best friend and gets away with it.

The next day, Jacob tried kissing me while we were standing in line for lunch. I was so distracted and grossed out by him, I almost missed Jaxson's reaction to the whole ordeal.

He walked straight up to Jacob and punched him in the nose. Instantly, blood shot out of his nostrils, spraying everything in close range, including Jaxon and me. It was incredibly disgusting, but hilarious at the same time.

Jax and I looked at each other, taking in the scene around us, and burst into laughter. At that moment, he came to my rescue, my knight in shining armor. Sealing our bond in blood. Jax and I, well, we're a special kind of crazy.

After that, things kinda fell into place. They accepted me into the group, and the guys quickly became my whole world. And if I'm being honest, over time, I started developing feelings for them. Dreams of being more than friends. Ideas that I try to shut down as they creep up.

Rarely do I let these fleeting thoughts slip into my mind. I know how devastating it would be if my true feelings were revealed. If I'm lucky, they'll live and die only in my mind because the alternative means choosing, and there's no way I could ever choose between the guys. They all tug at my heart strings in different ways.

That's not to say I haven't had earth-shattering moments with each of the guys because I have. Well, all of them except for Dante. He's made it a point to keep me in the friend-zone.

The summer going into our sophomore year, Jaxon gave me my first real kiss. It wasn't a quick peck on the lips. No, it was a toe-curling, make your body come alive kind of kiss.

It was during a game of truth or dare. Lucky had dared Jaxon to kiss me, and I started giggling assuming that he would never do it.

We all learned to never dare Jax to do anything. He will follow through every time. Jax quickly jumped up and grabbed my hands, pulling me up with him. He leveled me with a look filled with determination. His eyes were asking a question that only I could understand.

He looked like a god standing there staring down at me. Even at sixteen, he was rippled with muscles, short, dark hair, and his eyes were gray with a sparkle that rivaled diamonds. He'd just started working on his tattoos and they were already drool worthy.

I had never realized how much I wanted to kiss Jaxon Rivers until that moment. The butterflies in my stomach fluttered like little maniacs trying to escape. My heart was beating so fast I thought it would explode out of my chest. Jaxon was patient. He didn't make a move until my head nodded slightly, giving him a subtle yes.

With one hand, he grabbed me by the hip, while the other drifted up into my hair, twisting his fingers at my roots and tugging me to him. His body was warm, his embrace was strong.

The smell of his cologne sent a flood straight down to my lady bits.

The moment our lips touched, I saw stars. I felt his tongue brush against my lips as I opened up for him. It danced the most seductive dance inside my mouth. that, along with the slight tugs of my hair, had my whole body tingling with excitement.

Goosebumps erupted all over my entire body. Everything south of the border was aching with need in a way I had never felt before.

Was it possible to steal a piece of someone's soul through their mouth? Because I'm sure that's exactly what he did to me. He stole a piece of my soul with a single kiss.

Lost in his touch, the world and everyone around me faded to black. My moment of bliss was quickly stolen when Royal decided to ruin it before things could get too hot and heavy.

My mind was drifting somewhere between Heaven and la-la land while my body tagged along for the ride. Suddenly, Jaxon flew from my arms, and my lips were left cold and hollow.

When I finally found the strength to open my eyes, Royal's piercing glare could have set me ablaze. He looked at me with such disdain, or maybe it was jealousy. I don't know for sure, but I didn't like it either way.

It was probably a good thing the kiss didn't last more than a second. My stomach twisted into knots at the thought of what the guys had just witnessed. I didn't mean to be so consumed by his touch.

Royal immediately turned his attention from me to Jaxon and Lucky. He began yelling at Lucky for being dumb enough to give Jax that kind of dare, *knowing* he would never back down. Lucky just shrugged his shoulders like he didn't have a care in the world.

Then Royal turned his rage on Jax. He was furious. He started shoving Jax away from me, but Jax stood his ground. Dante and I quickly moved to separate the two of them before Royal pushed Jaxon too far. There would be *no* coming back from that.

Dante and I formed a barrier between them. I was screaming at Royal to stop. Telling him that it was just a stupid dare, that the kiss didn't mean anything. But he knew better, and the look he gave me as he shook his head and stormed off said he didn't believe a word that came out of my mouth. Hell, with the way my body was feeling, even *I* didn't believe the lies I was spewing.

A few months later, we were at a party when someone suggested we play Spin the Bottle.

Royal and I were the only two playing from our group. It took me by surprise that he even wanted to play such a silly game. Normally, he leaves the games to Jax, Lucky and myself, but it made me happy he decided to let loose and have some fun. He's always so serious and chose to play babysitter to the rest of us at these parties.

When it was my turn, it landed on one of the football players from our school who was sitting beside Royal. Before the guy had a chance to make a move, Royal reached down and shifted the bottle so that it pointed to him.

No one dared to say a word about him cheating as he looked like he could murder you with a simple stare. He was dark and broody, towering over the others at six-foot-four. His short, dark, faded haircut gave off military vibes. His beard had already formed along a jawline that could slice glass, and his piercing ice blue eyes carried a dark and seeded past. He couldn't be scarier if he tried, which made him even sexier to me.

I couldn't help the mischievous grin that spread across my face, smiling from ear to ear and giving him my best come-hither eyes.

Royal James pulled me into the second soul-consuming kiss of my life. If he hadn't been holding me so tightly against his body, I would have collapsed on the floor the instant my knees gave out. Royal's kiss was possessive and demanding. He was claiming my mouth for his own.

Royal swiftly broke our kiss, leaving me panting for more. He knew what he was doing, and I wanted to smack that cocky-ass grin off his face.

Still holding me tight, he stared into my eyes, or rather the depths of my soul, then threw me a wink as he walked away. That was the beginning and the end of the game for us.

After the party was over, Lucky and I decided to walk home since it was in our neighborhood. He walked me up to my door and, with no hesitation, leaned down and kissed me. I thought I was going to burst from the lust overwhelming and filling me up. The lingering feeling from Royal's kiss was still very much present, and Lucky was pushing me right over the edge.

My sweet, sweet Lucky Newman took me by surprise. He was the golden boy of our group.

Tall, with blonde wavy hair. Sun-kissed skin, broad shoulders, and large muscles that made him look like the epitome of a surfer boy. His deep, green eyes sparkled like emeralds. He was the only one of the guys who hadn't gotten any tattoos. He was my Lucky, and he was perfect.

His kiss was fierce. Once again, I was caught up in the moment while his hands explored my body. They moved along my curves, igniting my skin with every touch. I was insatiable. I couldn't get enough of him. That was until someone started clearing their throat, causing us to break apart in a hurry.

Lucky's younger sister, Cassie, started laughing like a little schoolgirl, and took off to their house next door. I looked up at Lucky, twisting his shirt in my fingers and pulling him back to me.

He chuckled but gave in to my needy self as he kissed me for a second longer. When he opened my door for me and said goodnight once more, I knew these boys would bring me to my knees. They could make me or break me, and I no longer had a say in the matter. My heart belonged to them.

My brain filled with forbidden thoughts after that night. I didn't know if it meant anything more to them, but it did to me, and that idea was just insane. It wasn't as if I could be with all of them, no matter how much I wanted that.

I found myself craving to be near them, starving for their attention. Every second we spent apart made me crazy. I needed them like I needed oxygen. Each one of their kisses left me starving for more, but I couldn't shake this nagging feeling of guilt. I didn't want just one of them. I wanted all of them, and I could feel it in my soul that they wanted me too.

My thoughts consumed me for months. I was confused, indecisive, and drowning in my feelings. I had never kissed anyone other than them, and it didn't help the situation that I had nothing to compare it to, just a needy desire flowing through me.

I realized I couldn't pursue anything with any of them because it would inevitably tear us apart. I couldn't be with one without hurting the others and I would never willingly do that. So, I put those feelings in a box and threw away the key.

Friends. That's all we could ever be, and I had to be okay with my decision.

As long as they were in my life and by my side, things would be alright. As long as they were by my side, I could move on or so I thought.

During our senior year of high school, Gabriel, Dante's dad, took over as President of the Sons of Diablo MC. That's when our lives drastically took a turn for the worse. Gabriel always had quite the mean streak, so we stayed clear of him as much as possible. He never paid much attention to Dante, but when he did, it wasn't the kind of attention that any kid would want.

The only thing that mattered to him was the Sons and grooming Dante to follow in his footsteps, teaching him the things we didn't learn in school, and showing him a lifestyle most children shouldn't know. He would even make him fight with members of the Sons to toughen him up. But through it all, one thing remained true, Gabriel's thirst for power.

Once Gabriel became the president, he suddenly wanted to know everything. Who Dante was with, where he was, and what he was doing.

Which was crazy, considering when we were little he didn't even bother to make sure there was food on the table.

Royal was the lucky one. The rest of us either had no father in the picture or drew the short stick, like Dante. Royal's father, King, was a member of the Reapers of Havoc MC. He looked after all of us, made sure we had clothes, food, school supplies, and whatever else we needed that our moms couldn't afford.

Lucky and I didn't have dads, we had sperm donors who took off when we were little. They couldn't handle the responsibility of being parents. Jaxon's dad is dead, and Gabriel just doesn't care.

King was good to us and never asked for anything in return, except for us to stay out of trouble. However, we never held up our end of that bargain. Since we were all hellions, trouble followed us everywhere.

From Royal's stories, his dad was motivated and quickly worked his way up through the club. Shortly after Gabriel took over the Sons, the Reapers' pres. was gunned down.

Everyone in town knew who was responsible, but there was no evidence to prove it. Whether Gabriel did the deed himself or put a price on his head, he had a hand in his death.

That's when King was voted in as President of the Reapers.

After Gabriel took over the Sons, our quiet town of Imperial Beach, California, wasn't so quiet anymore. He used his new position in the MC to start turf wars with the Reapers. From the very beginning, Gabriel was pushing boundaries. He was always trying to provoke the Reapers. Never caring who got hurt in the process.

As long as it benefited him and his need to gain more power or territory, then he was all for it.

He slowly started making excuses as to why Dante couldn't hang out with us. Then, right before our graduation, he put a stop to us hanging out completely. He told Dante that he had to start grooming him to take over the MC one day, which was the last thing Dante wanted to do with his life.

Devastated doesn't even begin to describe how we felt when he forced Dante away from us. It's been two years since I have seen my friend.

The few times we tried to sneak off somewhere, Dante always paid the price for it in blood. Dante would stay away from us until his bruises started healing up, but he couldn't fool me.

I knew they were there by the yellowing of his skin and the way he'd grimace when I hugged him.

He wouldn't talk to us about what Gabe was doing to him, but we knew it was bad. I hated seeing him like that and not being able to help him or understand what he was going through. It killed me. I could see the fear and the lost look in his eyes. That look tore me apart every time I saw it.

After a while, we just stopped trying to hang out. It was hard on us to see our friend so broken when he loved so deeply and took care of everyone. I think something broke inside him each time he had to leave us, but what hurt the worst was when he stopped responding to our calls and texts.

Having a piece of your heart ripped away isn't something I would wish on my worst enemy. Since then, the rest of us have been inseparable, clinging to every moment we have with one another.

What scares me the most is the thought of losing any one of them. For two years now, that thought has haunted my nightmares. I wouldn't be able to handle that, and I don't think they would be able to either.

Which is why my current situation is blowing my fucking mind.

Chapter Two

ANGEL

Stopping myself from dwelling on the past any longer, I try to focus on the present. I really wish life hadn't led me here, but there's nothing I can do about it now. So, stalking it is.

Relief fills me as I spot King and a few other members pulling into the clubhouse.

It's now or never.

Making my way across the street, I holler out to grab King's attention.

"King. Where the hell are they? It's been a week already, and this shit is getting old."

Okay, that may have come off a little too sassy.

King turns around, leveling me with a look filled with irritation.

Oh, shit!

This man has known me most of my life, so he also knows that my mouth has a tendency to get me into far too much trouble.

I always thought he liked my take-no-shit personality. It's also possible that he just finds my attitude funny when it's not directed at him. King doesn't allow disrespect from anyone, and I'm now certain that "anyone" also includes me.

"Angel, what an unpleasant surprise. What brings you by?" he mocks, throwing his hands up in the air.

"Really, King? Stop with the theatrics. Playing dumb doesn't suit you," I snort.

"First off, watch your damn mouth, little girl. I ain't one of your little boyfriends. When you speak to me, it will be with some respect." His brow furrows. "Second, *my* boys are gone. I don't know when they'll be back. Club business. Nothing you need to worry your pretty little head about. So, don't waste your time coming back around here. I'm sure they'll let you know *if* they return." His dismissive words are like ice to my veins.

"What do you mean, if? Why the fuck wouldn't they return?"

"Enough. I'm done with the questions, Angel. Go home. Stay away from the club for a while. It's not safe," King states.

I roll my eyes unwilling to accept that answer.

I'm a few seconds from losing my damn mind, and that won't be good for anyone. Why is he treating me like a total stranger?

"Seriously, King, that's all I get? I thought we were family."

King snatches my arm in his grip, squeezing hard enough to leave a bruise. He drags me to the side so that the other club members can't hear us. "You thought wrong. Listen up, Angel. I'm only saying this once. Stay. Away." His grip tightens, making me wince in pain.

"The boys are gone and won't be coming home anytime soon. Don't you think if they wanted you to know where they were, they would've told you? So, maybe you should make some new friends to play with instead of sitting outside my clubhouse all damn day and night like a lost, little mutt. The clubhouse is no place for a girl like you anyway. I should never have allowed it in the first place. All you've done is distract them from their responsibilities and that stops now." I stare at him in disbelief. His words are harsh and cut deep.

Someone please tell me this is not happening. While the earth keeps spinning, my world is crashing down. It takes a few seconds before the shock wears off. I finally snap out of it, gathering the courage to say what I need to.

"Fuck you, King. They're my best friends, and I deserve to know where they are and if they're in trouble. I need to know that they're okay, and you're the only asshole with the information."

King shakes his head at me as his eyes fill with guilt, but when he blinks, it's gone, leaving nothing but anger staring back. "Get the hell out of here before I have you physically removed, Angel. You're no longer welcome in the company of the Reapers. I'm sure you'll thank me one day."

Wow, so he went there. Pulling my arm out of his grip, I spin on my heels and walk away, lifting my middle finger toward the sky as I reach my Ducati. I see a few guys' eyes bulging out in shock, whipping their heads toward King. They're waiting for a reaction that never comes.

He makes his way to the clubhouse entrance like he doesn't have a care in the world.

King gives off this super scary vibe to everyone around him. I get it. He has a reputation to uphold. He's dangerous when it comes to the club and protecting Imperial Beach but he's never treated me like an outsider. I've been around the club my whole life and now he just expects me to walk away because what? He says so?

No, I don't think so.

He knows what the guys mean to me, and he should understand that this is tearing me apart. I know he's a good man at heart, but it doesn't stop me from throwing my middle finger high in the sky, waving it around for all the Reapers to see. Maybe it's a little immature, but I don't give two flying fucks. I want my boys and I want them now.

For whatever reason, King is standing in the way of the guys coming home to me. My instincts are telling me the guys are in trouble, and I won't stop until I find out what's really going on.

Chapter Three

LUCKY

One week ago

"Hey, King just called. He says he has a job for us and needs us to meet him at the clubhouse in a few hours," Royal says as he sits down beside me on the park bench. We're watching Jaxon and Angel work their magic, tagging the side of a building with the Reapers' logo. They're just asking for trouble.

"We can head over to the clubhouse when they finish here. We'll drop Angel off on our way," Royal says.

"They're going to get busted one of these days. And you, my man, are going to be the one who has to bail them out. You know that, right?" I laugh, patting him on the back.

Royal chuckles as he raises his brows, giving me the side-eye. "Yeah, sure, Luck. You'd just let them rot in jail. Real believable, bro. Don't act like I'm the only Captain Save-A-Ho around here. You play the part perfectly when it suits you. Besides, they're having fun and Jax needs to blow off some steam after his run-in with the Sons last night. This is good for him," Royal retorts, throwing shade in my direction.

He's right, Jax had one hell of a night. And being around Angel always seems to calm our crazy.

It's like she's the demon whisperer or some shit. She really is our Angel in more ways than I can count.

Last night, after Jax dropped Angel off at home, shit went sideways. He stopped at the corner store to pick up some stuff his mom needed, and all hell broke loose.

Four members of the Sons of Diablo rolled up on him, recognizing his bike outside of the store. They thought they'd catch him slipping. What they failed to realize was that Jax is one crazy motherfucker, and their numbers don't scare him.

Jax was walking out of the store with the groceries when they blindsided him.

They got him pretty good too, but Jax gave as good as he got. It was still four against one, and even outnumbered, my money is always on Jax no matter the odds.

Thankfully, he was quick to knock out the first two that came for him. Jax is crazy when he needs to be, and it almost makes me feel sorry for the fuckers. Almost. One of the two remaining guys pulled a knife, slicing Jax's stomach and arms. He fought off those last two guys and eventually convinced them to stay down long enough to hop on his bike and get the hell out of there. He headed straight to the clubhouse to get patched up.

Royal and King were still there when Jax walked in, bleeding everywhere.

King was furious. He called a meeting early this morning to discuss retaliation. This war between the Sons and the Reapers is never ending.

The moment we start to relax and think things have died down, shit pops off again. Something is always fanning the flames and adding fuel to the fire. It's an endless cycle of death and destruction. Sometimes, I wonder if it's even all worth it.

The Sons of Diablo fight dirty. Always have, but even more so since Gabriel took over as their leader. He's out for Reaper blood and will stop at nothing to get it.

He's the scum of the earth. The guy has no morals. He doesn't live by any kind of code. He sure as hell doesn't have any boundaries. Motherfucker is dark and twisted. I could never follow a guy like that into battle. I sure as fuck wouldn't call him my pres. At least with King you know he has your best interest at heart and that he'll always look out for you.

I don't know who thought it would be a good idea to make Gabriel President of the Sons, but they had to be higher than a kite. The guy barely looked after his own kid. What made them think he could lead a whole MC?

If it weren't for Gabriel being Dante's father, King probably would have put a bullet between his eyes a long time ago, but King has a soft spot for Dante. I know he thinks he's doing it for Dante's benefit, or maybe he has other reasons. Regardless, I think Dante would welcome Gabriel's death without question.

We know Gabriel and the Sons are into some shady shit. King has even tried turning a few members of the Sons by offering them a true brotherhood, but as soon as they agree to King's terms, they end up missing or dead.

Gabriel is smart, he knows what he's doing. I'll give him that much. The psycho leaves their bodies in the streets for the other Sons, and their families, to discover. He's sending them a message. For the most part, it's worked. He has them all scared to even look our way.

Anyone who questions his authority or tries to get out of the Sons meets his wrath. It's primarily lower-level members who thought they were signing up for a life of camaraderie and brotherhood. Instead, they ended up with that twisted fuck as a leader.

We hear the rumors. They say he threatens their ol' ladies and their kids. Like I said, the man has no boundaries. Nothing is off the table for him, which puts everyone in this town on edge.

The Sons of Diablo's counsel are just as toxic, which helps Gabriel keep the other club members in line. Cut the head off of one beast, and seven others appear. King will find a way to bring him down. Hopefully, sooner rather than later. It's all about timing.

The sun is starting to set as Jax and Angel finish their badass Reapers mural. Jax spray painted the skull while Angel put her twist on it. She added roses in all different shades of purple and topped it off with her signature angel wings on the side. It's the same design they've been tagging across town since we decided to join the Reapers. I'm sure the owner will thank us later.

Jaxon hops up on the park bench full of energy while Angel throws herself across Royal's lap and lays her head in mine as if she's exhausted from wreaking havoc on the side of this poor building. She's spoiled rotten, and she knows it.

I lean down, kissing her forehead. "Are you tired from all of your hard work, Trouble?" I ask.

She dramatically throws an arm over her head. "Exhausted, sugar tits."

"What's the plan for the rest of the night? I've worked up quite an appetite. Do y'all wanna grab something to eat?" she asks, wiggling her eyebrows at me.

"Well then, we must feed our hard-working woman," I proclaim, lifting her off my lap. "Come on Angel, spread your wings. The boys and I need to head over to the clubhouse. We'll feed you and drop you at home. You know, so that you can get your beauty sleep."

"Are you saying I need beauty sleep, Lucky? Because if you are, we're going to have problems," she asks with her hands on her hips, giving me her best mean face, but it doesn't look mean at all. It's pretty fucking adorable if you ask me.

I laugh at her failed attempt to intimidate me, causing her to slap my arm. She knows she's the most stunning woman ever. She's five foot nothing with the curves of a goddess, long blonde hair, and the face of an angel to match her name. She has the most delicious-looking plump lips that I've been dying to taste again. With her high cheekbones and soul-piercing blue eyes, Aphrodite has nothing on my girl.

"I would never say such a thing," I respond clutching my chest pretending to be offended by her accusations. "I still remember the last ass-whooping you gave me, Trouble. My balls are still recovering."

She whips her hair around and looks at me over her shoulder. "Good, I'd hate to mess up that pretty face of yours," she responds, baring her claws at me with a chuckle.

Royal gets up grabbing Angel's hand, and begins walking toward the parking lot.

"Come on, let's go, Princess. King is waiting, and we need to get you home. You're riding with me," he says.

Angel folds her arms across her chest, pouting and pushing her breasts up. I love it when she pouts.

"Can't you guys call in sick? I don't want to spend all night by myself."

"I wish it worked that way, Trouble. I'd call in sick every night to be alone with you," I say, giving her a sexy little wink, which results in her throwing her head back and laughing at me.

"Don't blow smoke up my ass, Luck. I know you'd rather be at the clubhouse with all the easy skanks—oops, I mean *hangarounds*," she spits, turning to look at Jax. "Jax, how many whores has Lucky slept with this week?"

I rapidly shake my head at him from behind her back. Jax better keep his mouth shut on this one. What Angel doesn't know can't hurt her.

Jax chuckles, "Nope, not happening, Trouble. You and Lucky keep your lovers' quarrel between the two of you. Don't bring me into it." *Good answer, man. He's smarter than he looks I tell ya.*

"Okay then, Jax, how many have you slept with this week?" she snaps with an evil glare.

Apparently Royal has had enough of this conversation because he grabs Angel by the waist, picks her up, and places her on the back of his bike.

"Enough of that, Princess. We all know you don't want the answers to those questions," he says as her playfully vicious mood instantly falters.

"Who says I don't?"

"I do! And we all know it, so stop trying to start shit for the hell of it," Royal responds.

Angel's face drops immediately.

"Wow, who knew you were all such whores? Oh wait, that's right. I did." She tries to joke, but I can hear the hurt in her voice. I hate it. It makes my stomach sink so I try and lighten the mood the only way I know how.

"Come on, Trouble, don't be like that. You know we'd all jump your bones in a heartbeat and never look at another woman again, but then Royal and Jax would get all butthurt when you picked me over them. We don't want that, now do we?" I say, but it falls flat. It wasn't amusing but mainly because it's true and still stings to know that she'll never truly be mine the way I want.

We would all kill for the chance to be with her, but that would never happen. She looks con-

"We're right on time. Take a chill pill, VP," I say, throwing my arm over Cruz's shoulder like we are best friends.

Cruz looks like I grew another head as he grabs my arm and throws it off his shoulder. He looks at the three of us and then back at King. "If you're on time, then you're late. What have you been teaching these knuckleheads, King?" Cruz says.

King laughs. "Apparently, not enough. Maybe you need to teach them a few lessons on time-liness and respecting your elders."

Cruz chuckles. "We're thirty-eight. I'm not ready to be considered an elder just yet."

"Boys, we have an important shipment coming in from the cartel." King's mood gets serious as he addresses us. "We need to secure the transport across state lines, and then our job is done. "We need to head out soon to get set up in time. We don't need any fuckups. So, I want everyone to be on their toes tonight. There's no room for error here." King looks around the room making eye contact with each of us.

"Shadow is already doing recon on the best route to take. He'll send me the meeting point once he knows it's safe," Cruz chimes in.

King nods and looks back at us. "If you see anything suspicious or anyone looking for trouble, then we need to know immediately. Everyone is getting a radio, and we ride in pairs. If your partner goes down, then your ass better be right beside him, or there will be hell to pay. No man left behind, got it? Any questions?"

"Got it," we reply in unison.

"Good, now get inside and strap up. We ride out in fifteen minutes," King orders.

I slap a hand down on Jax and Royal's shoulders. "Stay strapped or get clapped, boys." They chuckle at me as we head toward the weapons room. We get what we need and head back outside to our bikes.

"It's going to be a long night, fellas. Let's ride," King says before taking off.

We have a two-hour ride to the border. Royal and I are riding side by side, with Jax and Sinner behind us. There's no one better to watch your six than those two crazy fuckers. Club life can get wild at times, but it's the only life I know.

Now, I just need my patch.

Each prospect needs a sponsor to be patched into the club. They take responsibility for you. If you fuck up, it's on them. If you choose not to follow orders, they're responsible for a suitable punishment.

King refused to sponsor us because it would look biased, so Sinner is sponsoring Jaxon, while Shadow stepped up for me.

Cruz offered to sponsor Royal, and that's good because Cruz has a good head on his shoulders. That's why he's the VP. He's always level-headed when shit goes sideways, which happens more often than not lately.

Cruz is an ex-marine, and after three tours in the desert, he came home and found his ol' lady cheating on him. The crazy bitch stole all of his money and left him with nothing. That's when he decided to join the Reapers.

Sinner and Shadow are brothers and two of the craziest, twisted-ass men you'll ever come across. They're on another level of psycho. I never want to see the other side of them.

They've seen and dealt with some messed up shit in their lives, but they don't speak about it.

If it's not about the club, then you don't hear them talk about anything. They keep to themselves outside of the Reapers.

Shadow is the Reapers' Sergeant-at-Arms, deadly quiet and moves like the wind. He's snuck up on me so many times that I'm surprised I haven't pissed myself by now.

Shadow and I are complete opposites. I'm loud and can admit to being obnoxious sometimes. I have a hard time knowing when to keep my mouth shut. I blurt out whatever pops into my head.

Hmm, I never thought about this. Maybe Shadow is trying to teach me a lesson about stealth, or maybe it's the whole "opposites attract" thing. Who knows, but I'm fucking grateful to have him looking out for me.

Sinner is the Reapers' Road Captain. He always has this crazy look in his eyes, and the things I've seen him do to a man would give you nightmares.

They even gave me nightmares... Crazy bastard.

Sinner and Jax as a pair, now that makes a little more sense. They're both crazy as hell. Jax with his trauma and Sinner with his, they're two peas in fucked up pod.

Focusing on the road, I think about tonight's run. I'm hoping everything goes smoothly, and we can quickly get back to Angel.

King made a deal with the Castro Cartel to help run guns across the Mexican border to

Cali. It brings in money for the club, and so far, there have been no hiccups. So fingers crossed.

In a few short hours, I'll be sneaking into Angel's room for snuggles and back rubs.

Chapter Four

JAXON

One Week Ago

Three hours later, we're paying our tickets at a diner in the middle of nowhere. Cruz and King have their heads together out front, and Shadow pulls us aside as we're heading out to join them. "The route looks clear, barely any cops through town, and the back roads were pretty much deserted," he informs us, turning quickly without waiting for a response and straddling his bike.

The seven of us take off, heading to the rendezvous point. It's been a real struggle for me to focus on the job. My mind keeps replaying the events of last night over and over. I can count on one hand how many people have caught me off guard like that, and it didn't end well for them.

There are so many things that I should have done differently, but I shouldn't be dwelling on that now.

Last night, Angel consumed my mind, and that's what got me into trouble. It was a sloppy move on my part. No one to blame, but myself for that.

Part of me is glad it was me and not one of the other guys. They can all handle their own when it comes to a fight, but I was born into the darkness. There was no light in my life until Angel came along and saved me.

I've been beaten bloody more times than I can count.

I've battled monsters for as long as I can remember.

The pain is just part of who I am now.

The demons found me too easily when I was just a child, and even as I entered adulthood, I had to deal with evil men my whole life. My dad being the worst of them all. I can spot the demons stirring in someone a mile away, and I know exactly how to put them down.

Life has always been challenging for me, but I've managed to push through. Being around the guys and Angel seems to help. She's the best part of my day, and maybe even the best part of me.

When we were little, Lucky would bring her along everywhere we went, and I hated it.

Hated her.

She was like his shadow following us around everywhere we went.

Then one day Jacob what's-his-face tried kissing her in the lunch line one day, and all I saw was red. I didn't know what came over me, but how dare he try to kiss her. She wasn't his to touch, and he had to learn that lesson the hard way.

I punched him in the nose and sent him crying to his mommy.

From that day forward, Angel was mine to protect. I would make sure she had a good life, one that didn't reflect mine in any way.

My home life was shit, so I spent every moment I could with my friends. My parents were the last people I wanted to be around. They didn't seem to care if I was there or not anyway, so it worked out for all of us.

My mom I think she tried to love me, at least in her own way. Maybe she even cared for me at some point, but my father was an evil man who wanted her full attention and she gave it to him.

Even at the expense of her own child.

He was a possessive alcoholic who liked to beat on us. He would get pissed at Mom for not giving him enough attention or if he felt like she was spending too much time playing with me.

I think he resented me for being alive, not that I had much of a choice in the matter, but that didn't stop him from taking all his anger out on me and my mom.

My friends were my sanctuary, my safe haven away from the hell that awaited me at home. The only time I could be myself was when I was with them.

Angel and I were always causing trouble. Dennis the Menace had nothing on us. All the others were scared to get in trouble with their parents, but not Angel. She wasn't scared of anything.

They would all sit back, laugh, and watch us unleash our mayhem.

When we decided to join the Reapers, we had already lost Dante to his father, and we didn't want Royal joining alone. So, we decided to patch with him to keep what was left of our family intact. The only problem with that was, I'm not cut out for a life of following orders.

I had enough of that as a child.

Unfortunately, that's my primary job as a prospect, following club orders. So, I bite my tongue and hope for the best most days.

Don't even get me started on how much time it takes away from being with Angel which drives me insane.

All the nights I could be spending with her, but instead, I'm out doing runs for the club. Sure, it pays the bills and puts food on the table, so I try to suck it up for the most part, but it's not what I want to do.

I hate leaving her every time we have a job, but Royal keeps telling us to just grind it out. He says things will be different once we have our patches, but I don't see how. If anything, we will be handling even more business for the club when that time comes.

Angel would be by our side if she were allowed, but the club would never let a woman become a member. I wonder if she'll consider being my ol' lady one day.

I laugh at that thought, knowing it will never happen, but a man can dream, right?

Angel would never bow down to a man, or the club, or anyone for that matter. No, she is a force to be reckoned with.

I know she was still worried about me when I dropped her off, although she did her best to hide it and distract me today.

My life has never been sunshine and rainbows. Nope, I was raised in the pits of hell, surrounded by demons trying to steal my soul. It's not the life I would have wished for, but it's the one I was handed.

The four of us have known each other for so long that we're all in sync with one another.

Lucky has a smile plastered on his face constantly, always making us laugh and forget whatever is going on around us.

Royal can see right through our souls, knowing exactly what we need and when we need it. He's a true leader through and through.

Dante had this way of accepting us for who we were, never judging, just loved us unconditionally. Man, I really miss my brother.

Angel is the better half of me and gets me without me having to say a word. She knows when to pull me from my dark thoughts or when I need to just let loose and have some fun. She keeps my demons on a leash and knows when to set them free. She is the air I breathe, and no one will take her from me. She's my only vice, my sweet obsession, and the purest form of ecstasy for my twisted soul.

They all give me a reason to keep going, something to believe in.

As we pull up to the meeting point, I see the cartel in front of the semi-truck we have to escort over the border. King hops off his bike, says a few words to them, and heads back in the direction we just came.

King, Sinner, and Royal are riding in the front. Shadow, Lucky, Cruz, and I are riding behind the truck.

We need to hurry and get this job done so I can get back to my girl before my thoughts spiral into darkness again.

I need my anchor, but she's nowhere near to pull me out of this.

I remind myself that I will be with her soon. I just need to keep it together for a bit longer.

We're in the middle of nowhere, going as fast as we can to get this truck across the border without getting popped by the cops.

Sure, we have some local cops on the Reapers payroll, but that doesn't do us any good way out here.

Riding through the hills in the backwoods of Cali, coming up to the top of yet another mountain, I see the red and orange colors lighting the sky. As we reach the top, fear seeps in as I see the flames stretching across the entire road and into the trees on both sides.

It's a fucking trap!

The truck behind me is going too fast to stop before we reach the bottom. The truck driver must see it at the same time I do because I hear the squeal of the brakes, but it's too late.

King and Sinner swerve to the right trying to avoid the flames. Royal and I shift to the left, doing the same. I hear a popping sound from beyond the fire.

Bullets ricochet off the side of the truck as we get closer to the blaze at the bottom. The driver decides to step on the gas, making his way straight through the flames to the other side, but he collides with everything in his path. That's when I see the truck swerve off the road and slide to a stop.

Damn, they must have hit the driver.

I look back to see Cruz and Lucky heading toward me while Shadow veers toward King and Sinner. I draw my gun from its holster, preparing for what's coming next. There's nowhere to take cover unless we can get to the wooded area on the other side.

"We're sitting ducks out here. We need to move," Cruz says, coming up from behind me with his gun drawn.

He's right. We have no cover, and whoever this is will be picking us off one by one.

"Do we even know who's shooting at us?" Lucky asks, creeping around the front of his bike to take a few blind shots at whoever these assholes are.

"No, but Cruz is right. We can't just sit here. We don't even know how many of them are out there. We need to try to get that truck out of here, or we're going to have much bigger problems than this when the cartel finds out," I add. No one wants or needs the cartel coming after us.

They both nod their heads in agreement. We might be crazy, but we're not stupid. The Castro Cartel will drop the world on all of our heads if we don't hold up our end of the deal.

The flames are starting to die out, and they aren't as big as they were at first. So, we decide to make a run for it. Between the darkness and the smoke, it's hard to see the other guys from where we are. Hopefully, they're okay. I can still hear gunshots coming from that direction, so I'll take it as a good sign.

"Haul ass to the truck. Don't stop. Don't turn around. Once we have a little cover, we can figure out how to get that truck out of here. Just get to that fucking truck. Whatever it takes," Cruz demands.

I can hear the worry in his voice, but I need to focus on getting us out of here. My brothers need me to stay calm.

We hop on our bikes and speed off toward the semi. Shots ring through the air, and I can feel some bouncing off my ride, but the four of us make it to the truck with minimal damage.

"Shit, I only have one clip left," Cruz says, trying to hide the worry written all over his face. This is not looking good.

Men move around the sides of the truck, surrounding us. One guy swings at our heads with a machete, but Lucky kicks his feet out from under him and puts a bullet between his eyes.

From out of nowhere, I see Sinner in my peripheral, taking shots at these fuckers.

Bullets, knives, and hands are flying everywhere, and now we're fighting for more than just the cargo. We're battling for our lives.

I look over, noticing King locked in a fight with someone, going blow for blow. It's at that moment I realize just who this group is... *The Sons of Diablo.*

Gabriel and King are throwing heavy blows at one another, both of them fighting to be the alpha of this town. We're outnumbered, but I'm taking out as many of these fuckers as I can. If I go out, I'm doing it in a blaze of glory.

A behemoth of a man knocks Lucky to the ground as he grabs a knife from his belt and lunges toward him. I try to get to him, but Shadow beats me to it, shooting that fucker right in the face. The unlucky bastard swinging a knife at Sinner's chest has no idea what he's getting into. Sinner is thoroughly trained and lethal.

He twists the guy's arm, wrapping it around, making him jab the knife in the side of his own neck. Then he quickly pulls the guy's arm across his throat. Ouch, that had to hurt.

I'm out of bullets, so I use the butt of the gun to beat my attacker unconscious. Two others close rank around me. That's when I decide to let my monsters out to play. These guys are keeping me from my Angel, and I'll be damned if I die tonight.

Shadow and Sinner came prepared for war, picking these guys off left and right. They've taken out at least twenty men so far between just the two of them.

Royal is going head-to-head with a couple of guys, and I hear a gun go off. I'm not sure where the bullet came from, but Cruz must have. The next thing I know, Cruz is jumping in front of Royal and falling to the ground.

Rage takes over as I pull my knife from my boot. I'm slashing and stabbing everyone in sight. It's a bloody massacre out here. I look over to see Cruz crawling toward the bed of the truck for cover and I try to make my way to him in the midst of the chaos.

Royal becomes a beast, snapping necks like a fucking savage and shooting the ones he can't reach. He takes out five of the Sons within seconds.

Then out of nowhere, Royal aims for Viper, Gabe's second in command and his only blood brother. Without a second thought, he pulls the trigger. *Boom!*

Viper yells just before the gun goes off, causing Gabe to turn his head to watch his brother take his last breath on this earth. Gabe looks around, takes in the scene before him, and reaches for his gun.

Simultaneously, King and Gabe pull their guns and point them at one another, but neither of them make a move.

Gabe knows he's outnumbered. He looks toward the ground at all the slaughtered Sons of Diablo.

He created this war and look what it has cost him. How many men lost their lives tonight? And for what? Power? Control? He probably doesn't even know anymore.

"You're a dead man walking, boy," Gabriel growls at Royal.

"Take your men and leave while I'm feeling gracious," King spits. "It never needed to be this way. You wanted a war, and that's what you got. Now, you've lost your brother. A war between the clubs means we all lose. When will you see that?"

"Fuck you, King. You think your boy can kill my brother, and I'm going to let it slide? I must have hit you harder than I thought because you're fucking nuts if you think that's happening."

"I think you've lost enough men here tonight, Gabe. Your senseless escapades are growing tiresome. I'm allowing you to leave with your lives or stay and die here in the middle of nowhere. Which is it?"

"Don't fucking *Gabe* me." He shoves King, and I move forward, but King throws his hand up to stop me. "You lost the right to call me that years ago. Do your boys know what you did to me that started this war? To my family?" Gabriel looks at King viciously.

"That's enough, *Gabriel.* Take your men and leave before I change my mind," King orders.

"That's what I thought." He ignores King, and now I'm wondering what the fuck all that was about.

"Still quite the deceiver, I see."

Gabriel shakes his head as he makes his way over to Viper's body. He yells at the other Sons to help him put his brother on the back of his bike. Getting on himself, he turns toward us, saying something vague about taking the one we love, then takes off with his men in tow.

We rush over to Cruz, who's bleeding out propped against the truck.

"It looks worse than it is," he says, trying to calm us.

"Sinner, take the truck and the boys and get it to the border before anything else can happen tonight. Shadow, call Doc and tell him we're on our way, that Cruz has been shot," King orders.

"You will all meet me back at Doc's once you are finished. That's an order, no going to see your little girlfriend, no quick stops. Directly back to me. Is that understood?" We all nod in agreement.

It's going to be a long night.

Chapter Five

ANGEL

Present Day

After leaving the clubhouse, I pull into my driveway just as Cassie barrels out of her house sobbing. I hop off my bike and run down the street after her.

"Cass, wait up. What's going on?" I yell, trying to grab her attention. Hearing my voice, she suddenly stops, and her body drops to the ground while pulling her knees to her chest. I come to a stop in front of her and move to sit down beside her. We're both out of breath, but Cassie's breathing is more frantic than mine.

Crying and running is not a good mix, but shit, what's my excuse? I need to work out more, duh.

Cassie looks up at me with tears streaming down her cheeks.

"He's gone, Angel. I don't think he's coming back." My heart instantly drops into my stomach. I scoot closer to her, pulling her into my arms.

"My mom just spoke with him earlier, but he wouldn't give her any answers. He said that he was okay, but he was going to be gone for a while. I tried calling him back, but the number was disconnected. Their phones are cut off, and now we have no way of contacting them. What's going on, Angel? What could be so bad they can't come home?" All I can do is shake my head in disbelief. This can't be real.

"I wish I knew, Cass. I'm just as lost as you are about the whole situation. I've been camping in front of the clubhouse for days, hoping to see them. I saw King today, and he was no help. He and his big-dick energy can get fucked. He knows what's going on, but apparently, it's "club business" and no concern of mine. I'm not giving up just yet, Cass, so you shouldn't either."

Cass wipes her cheeks and turns to face me curiously. "You've been stalking the club-house?" she asks, bursting into laughter. "So, the rumors are true. You are a complete fucking psycho when it comes to the guys. Everyone said it was true, but I had a hard time believing it. I guess I just saw what I wanted to."

"I'll take that as a compliment, thank you."

"Well, it's not like it matters now, your psycho tendencies have gotten you nowhere. We still have no clue where they are," Cass whines and buries her face in her arms.

"Maybe I need a sidekick to help me. Think about it, two sets of eyes are better than one, and we can both do recon. When we find them, I'll let my crazy loose on them for all the hard work they made us do. You can join in for that part if you want." I quickly jump up and begin to karate kick and punch the air to show my crazy fighting skills, making us both burst out laughing.

I pull her up off the ground, and we start walking back toward our houses, both of us randomly throwing punches in the air. Anyone watching us would think we've lost our minds, and maybe we have, but you must find joy in the little things in life.

"I'll help you look for them, Angel. My friends act as if I should just get over it, but they don't understand. Without Lucky, our family is nothing. There's no normal or moving on without him. You get it. Mom and I can't survive without him. Hell, we can barely survive with him. What the hell are we supposed to do now?"

Cassie looks in my direction with tears swelling her eyes.

"I know you need answers, but I don't have the ones you're looking for, not today anyway." She holds my stare for a moment before looking away.

"I can see the pain in your eyes, Angel. You know how I feel better than anyone."

The words are stuck in my throat, so I nod instead of speaking. I hate that I feel this way. That I'm so dependent on them.

Feeling broken and empty is new to me. I'm not quite ready to admit to anyone how much I miss or need them.

I clear my throat before saying, "Come on, Cass, we can go crazy together." I smile, pulling her into my side and kissing her forehead. She's not wrong. I do get it.

Cassie is two years younger than me, but we have always been close.

She lives life to the fullest, and if she's feeling alone right now, then we can lean on each other to get through this.

We spend the next few weeks watching the clubhouse for any sign of the guys, but they never show up. My thoughts are getting darker, and hate is creeping into my heart. I never thought I would have to go through this again.

Yet here I am...

Losing Dante was one of the worst times in my life. For six months, I spent most of my days hiding away in my room. My mom was worried about me because I refused to come out unless it was to eat or if the guys dropped by. We were all hurting over Dante. I wanted to be there for them, but I couldn't get out of my own head to help them.

The guys tried their hardest to pull me out of it, getting me out of the house, taking me to parties, but life wasn't the same without him there with us. I don't want to go back down that road again, and I damn sure won't let Cassie sink into that kind of darkness.

You never realize how much you truly rely on a person, or in my case, people, until they're gone.

As much as it hurts, I have to get on with my life. I refuse to sit back and let life pass by. I've spent most of my life tethered to these guys, and until now, I never thought it was a bad thing. From here on out, I'll throw a smile on my face and fake it until I make it.

Three Months Later

Dead end after dead end. That's where our efforts got us. Week after week and day after day. Cassie and I got nowhere.

The first couple of months were the hardest, each day felt longer than the last without the guys.

After the first month passed it started to sink in, they didn't want to be found.

Month two, I was pissed. Filled with anger from their betrayal and lack of compassion for doing this to me. Leaving me here all alone, my life was ripped apart once more and I was left to pick up the pieces.

Slowly we started making a new normal for ourselves. Cassie and I got jobs at the Sunnyside Diner that's just a few blocks away from our houses. We spend most nights working and partying.

We drink our weight in alcohol every week and party until the sun comes up. All the while trying to make myself forget they ever existed.

We're both struggling but at least we are trying.

Trying to live our life and trying our hardest to fill the emptiness in our hearts.

It's Friday night, Cassie and I are working the night shift per usual, hyping ourselves up for a long night of partying. Last weekend when we went out, she ended up exchanging numbers with Ben, a random guy she made out with. He sent her a text earlier about going to a party on the north side of town in the Sons territory. Not my normal scene, but I'm down, like always, anything to numb the pain.

We finish our shift and head to my house to get ready.

After a quick shower, I throw on a skintight, sinfully short black dress that hugs my curves perfectly. Tossing half of my freshly dyed lilac hair up in a messy bun and curl the rest so it will fall down my back. I love the new color, and it makes me look fierce. I needed a change when the guys took off and so far it's working for me.

I look hot as fuck if I do say so myself. I grab a pair of knee-high boots to finish off my look as Cassie strolls out of the bathroom looking like straight fire.

"Damn, Cass. I sure hope that your new guy can fight. He's going to have his hands full trying to keep everyone's paws off you in that dress."

Cassie is a blonde bombshell with beautiful green eyes and legs that most women would kill for. She's the girl version of Lucky.

"Is it too much? Tell me the truth," Cassie asks, looking innocently into the mirror.

"Hell no, girl. You look good enough to eat."

"We are straight killin' the game tonight." Cassie gives me a booty bump as we take one last look in the mirror.

"Let's go, babe. Our driver just pulled up," I say, grabbing her hand and heading toward the door.

We always order a Lyft when we go out. I'm not going to risk crashing my bike for a night of partying, and I would never let Cassie drive drunk.

We pull up to the party a few minutes later and head inside. The music is blasting through the speakers in the living room. People are everywhere. They're dancing, drinking, dry humping, filling up any and all available space.

Making our way to the kitchen for a drink, we get so many nasty looks from the women along the way. Ignoring their glares, we keep walking.

Jealousy is such an evil little thing. I prefer building women up, not comparing myself to them and trying to tear them down. We all have our flaws, whether they are inside or out. Nobody's perfect, but some women are just too petty for their own good.

We get a couple of drinks in us, then head to the front room to dance. Ben comes up behind Cassie, grinding to the beat as one of his friend's hands out shots. We down them in one go, celebrating to new friendships and drunken nights.

We continue dancing in the front room, bodies pressed up against each other as the room becomes more crowded. I'm trying to get lost in the music when I get this weird feeling like someone is watching me.

My eyes drift around as I move my body to the music. I see nothing out of the ordinary so I decide to blame it on the alcohol and continue enjoying my night.

Everyone is dancing or trying to converse over the music when my skin starts to prickle.

This time I stop dancing and start scanning the room. It's crowded and my short stature doesn't help my visibility but I don't see anything out of the ordinary. So again, I try to shake the feeling.

I'm grinding my ass on some random guy when I start to get goosebumps all over my skin. Feeling the alcohol in my system, I spin around in the guy's arms and look around again. Hmm, nothing.

I turn around to find Cassie looking at me in confusion, but I just shrug. I have no idea what's going on with my senses tonight.

The guy I'm dancing with starts running his fingers up and down my body trying to cop a feel.

He's cute enough, but something about his hands all over me has me feeling icky.

I slide his hands back to my hips and he tries moving them down toward the hem of my dress.

Just as I step away from him to give him a piece of my mind, someone grabs his shoulder., yanking him away from me. Before I have a chance to blink someone punches him dead in the face.

And he goes down just like that.

I'm staring at the guy laid out at my feet when Ben steps in trying to defend his douchebag friend and then a full-blown brawl breaks out in the middle of the front room.

The next thing I know, everyone is pushing and shoving, knocking me further from the fight. I grab Cassie's hand, and we head to the backyard, snatching a bottle of rum on our way out.

A few minutes later, everyone starts clearing out of the house and the music picks back up. I'm assuming the drama is over now.

Cassie and I start dancing to the music in the backyard when it happens *again*. My body fills with heat as someone moves behind me, grinding his half-hard cock against my ass.

My body reacts instinctively, pushing back against him. Every sway of our bodies are in sync with the music and each other.

"Some things never change. Except, maybe your hair." The mystery man whispers in my ear while twirling a lock of my light purple hair in between his tattooed fingers. His body is still moving to the music, but I immediately freeze at the sound of his voice.

My heart stops and everything around me comes crashing down. *It can't be him.*

I turn around and stare into the beautiful deep blue eyes of Dante *fucking* Garcia.

Damn, he looks good—too good.

"Your boy's lucky it was me that saw him touching you like that and not one of your other boyfriends," he laughs. I'm dumbstruck. My brain and mouth are refusing to function. "He'd be in a shallow grave instead of just having a few bumps and bruises."

I must look like an idiot just standing here staring. Words, Angel. Use your words.

But I can't straight. It's been two fucking years since I laid eyes on him.

Two years since he walked away and never looked back.

He's even better looking than I remember, devastatingly handsome with his wavy brown hair, his ocean blue eyes, and his chiseled jawline. Built like a Greek god with a cascade of muscles and ink that make up his toned body.

Not too big, just big enough to pick me up and throw me around. *Get your mind out of the gutter, Angel.*

He hurt you! Stop drooling over the guy.

Cassie runs up from behind me, hugging Dante tight. "Always coming to Angel's rescue, huh, D?" she laughs, still holding onto him.

"Damn, Cass. Where's your bodyguard? Lucky let you out of the house looking like that?" he questions and Cassie's face drops at the mention of her brothers name. She gives him a tight-lipped smile taking a step back.

Dante must not notice her demeanor change because even though he's speaking to her, he hasn't taken his eyes off me.

Looking at me like he's ready to devour me. His deep baby blues are lighting my soul on fire. And all of a sudden, my body is burning up, my face is flushed. He licks his lips, which makes my pussy clench. Lust is pouring off us in waves.

Snapping out of my trance, I grab Cassie's arm to pull her away from him. Sure, he looks great, but that doesn't change the fact that he threw me out like yesterday's trash.

"Come on, Cass, you shouldn't talk to ghosts." She quirks a brow in my direction. "They don't exist, and people will think you're crazy." I say moving toward the house, but he snatches my arm, stopping me from my escape.

"C'mon, Heaven, don't be like that. I thought you would be happy to see me." He lets his nickname for me slip from his lips so quickly that it sends a shiver down my spine as our memories flood my mind—the good and the bad.

As much as I want to run into his arms, I can't.

He left me and never looked back. So, no. He doesn't deserve a warm welcome from me.

He deserves my wrath.

"Ghosts don't speak, and that's what you are. Now, fuck all the way off," I seethe, jerking my arm from his grip. Cassie grimaces at my harshness, but to be fair it isn't enough.

"I'm going to give you two a minute alone. It was nice to see you, Dante. We've *all* missed you," Cassie says, giving him another hug, throwing a wink my way before going back into the house.

She doesn't get it. Maybe she thinks I need this, but I don't. I've lost enough sleep over him and I'm not going back down that road. He made his choice and it wasn't me.

Before I can stop him, Dante takes my hand, pulling me toward his chest, and wraps his arms around me. Halfheartedly, I try to push him away, but letting myself fall into him. I've missed him so much. His embrace feels like home. The fight in me gives way, and I wrap myself around him.

"This is a dream, right? I'm going to wake up, and you'll be gone again. Leaving me with another Dante sized hole in my chest."

A single tear slips from my eyes, rolling down my cheek as I soak up his warmth. He smells so good, like leather and citrus, and his muscular arms wrapped around me make me feel so safe.

"I'm real," he breathes. "God, I've missed you, Heaven. I can't even begin to tell you how much I've longed for this."

Shaking my head into his chest, I push away from him. "No, I can't do this again. You broke me last time, and I won't ever let anyone do that to me again. Not even you, Dante. I've finally learned how to live life without you. You don't get to waltz back in, acting as if nothing happened. Like you didn't leave me and shatter my heart into a million pieces while doing it."

Dante looks confused and hurt by my rejection, but it is what it is.

"You think that's what I'm doing? Not everything is about you, Heaven. I came to a party on my side of town, never expecting to see you, but yet, here you are." He throws arms out wide in frustration.

"I'm not acting as if nothing has happened. This is me missing the fuck out of you for the past two years. You think I haven't thought about you every fucking day? You think it was easy just walking away from my best friends?

From you? Who the fuck do you think I am?"
He runs a hand through his short chocolate
hair.

"I know exactly who you are... Dante Garcia,
son of the devil himself. Daddy says jump, and
you ask how high? You left and never looked
back. As if our whole life together was just a lie,
a fucking afterthought to you. Like *we* meant
nothing to you." Okay, that might not be how
it exactly went down, but I'm drunk and pissed
off right now, so whatever!

"Clearly, you have had too much to drink
because you know that's not what happened. I'll
let you get back to your party though. I came
here to have a good time, not argue with your
delusional ass."

"Oh I'm the crazy one because you decided to
piss off and join your daddy's club. You abandoned your real brothers for them?" I shout.

"Yeah, so this conversation is pointless if
you're going to act like a brat and make shit up
in that thick ass head of yours." He moves his
arm, motioning toward the house as if telling
me that I'm free to go. Which I do.

"You're welcome, for saving your ass... *again*,"
he yells as I walk away from him.

"Fuck you, Dante Garcia. Fuck you." I throw my middle finger up at him as I enter the house, stopping to take another drink from the bottle of rum in my hand, then I head straight to the front room to get my dance on.

Chapter Six

DANTE

Seriously, who the fuck does she think she is? She's so damn frustrating. She shows up on my side of town and has the nerve to say I'm the one out of place.

I stayed away. I did precisely as Gabriel told me to.

Left and never looked back.

That's what he wanted, and that's what I did.

No matter how much it fucking hurt.

Gabriel can't be mad at me because she shows up out of nowhere.

Like I'm supposed to have some psychic power to know that she would be here tonight.

There's not a doubt in my mind that one of the Sons here with me tonight has already run their mouths to him about her being here. I'll deal with that when I get home tonight. I'm going to enjoy myself tonight because come tomorrow he will rain fire down on me. I'll never hear the end of his threats and be doing grunt work for a month.

Even after years of keeping my word to him, he still questions my every move, my loyalties, and just about everything under the sun he can think of.

If he only knew, I could never be loyal to a man like him.

Angel is right to call him the devil because that's exactly what he is, the devil in disguise. He may have the rest of the club fooled, but I know better. I see him, the real him—money-hungry, power-hungry, and pure evil.

Well, fuck it, I've waited too long for this opportunity, Carpe diem, motherfuckers. Tonight, I'm taking a piece of my life back. I'm not letting Angel get away that easily.

I walk back into the house, grab the first bottle of liquor I see, and start chugging it down. A little liquid courage never hurt anyone, right?

Scanning the crowd, I see another handsy motherfucker dancing with Angel, and my anger quickly rises to the surface. I move to her side, snatching her hand and pulling her away from the douchebag with a death wish. The guy looks at me like he's about to say something, then he must have second thoughts because he turns around and starts dancing with another girl.

Angel starts to walk away, but I grab her hips, pulling her ass right back to me.

She lets out a deep sigh but starts to sway to the music seductively, positioning her ass right against my dick as she does. She leans forward and bounces her ass up and down, moving it in circles against me.

Teasing me with every motion. My jeans are strangling my dick at this point, but it's worth it to feel her body grind on me.

My hands travel up and down her body, feeling the electricity coursing between us. Now grinding even harder, driving me crazy. I pull her up while putting my mouth right next to her ear so she can hear me.

"Don't start something if you aren't prepared to follow through, Heaven."

She cocks her head sideways to look at me as she chuckles. "My follow-through game is strong. Can't say the same for you, D."

So she thinks she has the upper hand, does she?

With every swirl of her ass against me, my resolve wavers more and more.

She's consuming me. I can't help myself. I dip my head and begin trailing kisses from her ear down her jawline, and then I move on to her neck. Goosebumps cover her body instantly. My hand moves from her hip to her stomach, holding her exactly where I want her.

I lick a path back up from her neck to her ear. "Then show me what you're working with, Heaven. I'm a big boy I can take it."

She chuckles spinning in my arms to face me. There's conviction in her eyes as she pushes me against the wall with one hand on my chest and looks me up and down.

"Is that what you want, Dante? To fuck me? Then what? Leave me, again?"

I scoff. "You're unbelievable. You seriously believe that shit?"

She shrugs, looking away from me.

"Fine, you wanna do this? Let's talk, but not out here." I take her hand, leading her to the back of the house.

I knock on a couple of doors that have people in them before finding an empty one. I pull her into the bedroom with me and lock the door behind us.

Angel looks hesitant but moves to sit on the edge of the bed, waiting for me to speak.

I start slowly pacing the room, wondering how the hell I can make this right. Knowing nothing I say will ever make up for what I've done.

"Angel, you have to know that I never meant to hurt you, or the guys for that matter."

She nods her head, looking down at her feet. "Doesn't make it hurt any less, Dante."

Slowly making my way to her, she looks up at me, tears filling her eyes. "I don't think I can do this again. I'm still trying to put the pieces of my life back together. All of you fucked with my head. You made me believe I was special just to turn around and rip my world apart in the end."

Wiping her tears away, she chokes out a sob that breaks me.

"You were my everything, even after you left us. But then, all that was left was your ghost haunting me in my dreams and torturing me in my nightmares."

"I'm so sorry, Angel. I wish I could take it back," I tell her. But do I? Would I? If it meant keeping her safe then I'd do it over again and again.

"Not a single phone call or text to let me know that you were okay. I don't understand how you could do that to me."

"I didn't have a—" She throws a hand in the air to silence me.

"I know it was Gabriel who forced your hand, but I'm not sure it changes the brokenness inside me. The nights I spent crying myself to sleep, wondering what he was doing to you. If you were hurt or even still alive. A simple phone call or text could have changed that. It wouldn't have made me stop missing you, but at least I would have had peace of mind that you were alright. Don't you get that?"

I nod my head in agreement because the lump in my throat is growing heavy. She's right. Every word she says is right. But I wasn't willing to risk it.

The only thing that kept me going on my darkest nights was knowing that even if Angel didn't have me, she had them. As her words sink in I wonder what else I'm missing here. "Why did you say we all fucked with your head? Where are the guys Angel?"

Something's happened. Lucky would never let Cassie come to a party on this side of town, looking like that. The guys would never agree to let Angel come here by herself or at all for that matter.

"Now's not the time, Dante. I don't want to talk about them."

"It's obvious something's happened so just tell me."

"Tonight is the first time I've set eyes on you in years. A huge part of me just wants to hold you so damn tight and never let go. But the other part of me wants to run screaming for the hills so that you can't break my heart again. I don't know what to do here. I never expected to see you tonight, but here you are, in the flesh."

I want to know what's going on with her and the guys but right now I need to fix things between us. This may be my only opportunity to tell her the truth without Gabriel knowing.

I've fucked up, and I need to make it right.

"Look, I know I fucked up. I'm not denying it. Everything I did, I did to protect you."

She rolls her eyes like she doesn't believe me.

"I let Gabriel control me out of fear. I lost the only family I ever had because of him. He may be my blood, but the four of you were my family."

I thrust a hand through my hair as I drop my gaze to the ground.

"For the last two years, I've had no one. The things he's made me do would make you never want to look at me again. Shit Angel, most days, I can't even look at myself." I let myself admit the reality of the situation for the first time.

I'm alone.

The people I love the most have moved on with their lives because I forced them too.

"Dante, the things you've had to do, that isn't who you are," she says, gripping the side of her dress to keep from reaching for me.

"I don't know who I am anymore. I'm fucking lost and drowning in this world. Everyone around me is loyal to Gabriel. They would turn on me in a heartbeat if he said so. My life is empty. I came here tonight hoping to get drunk and blow off some steam. Instead, I see some dickhead with his hands all over *my* fucking girl. Do you have any idea what that does to me? I wanted to rip his hands from his body. It drove me insane seeing him touch you."

Her eyes narrow, and a smile spreads across her face as she hops off the bed, moving toward me.

"Your girl?" she smirks.

She moves back to look up at me mischievously.

"My girl. My world. My joy and my pain. The air I *fucking* breathe. *Mine.*" Staring into her beautiful blue eyes is intoxicating, and I can't take the anticipation anymore.

Angel takes my hands and wraps them around her waist, pulling me into a hug and drawing circles on my back with her fingers. "I'm sorry, D. I'm sorry you've had to endure whatever hell he's put you through. I was drowning in my pain, and I didn't think about yours. I'm sorry you had to see that dickhead with his hands on me."

I grab her ass, lifting her off the ground as she wraps her legs around my waist, throwing her arms around my neck. I spin us around so her back is against the wall.

Our mouths collide. My need to consume her is overpowering. She pulls back, biting down on my bottom lip enough to draw blood. I feel the sting as she sucks it between her lips and pushes her tongue back into my mouth. I've never wanted someone or something as much as I do her.

I've waited so long to kiss her plump lips. She tastes sweet, like cherries and temptation. Her body is trembling as she grinds down on my dick, making it spring back to life. I'm not wasting a second of this opportunity. Tonight, she will finally be mine.

I pull us away from the wall and move toward the bed, placing her down on it and breaking our kiss. "Tell me what you want, what you need, Heaven, because I need to be inside you. I need to taste you, to claim every inch of you for myself. I want you to scream my name until everyone at this party knows who you belong to."

She moves back further onto the bed, spreading her legs, giving me a perfect view of her purple lace thong. A hungry growl escapes my throat as I begin to move my hands up her thighs and stop just before I reach her core. "Words, Heaven. I need the words."

She takes my hands, moving them away from her thighs and instantly filling me with disappointment. I feel like screaming. Then she lays flat on the bed, moving her hands to the hem of her panties, wiggling out of them, throwing them at my chest.

She leans up on her elbows, looking at the bulge in my jeans.

"You think you've got what it takes to claim me, Dante? Hmm, I don't know about all that, but I damn sure want to see you try."

Challenge accepted.

I take her ankle in my hand, moving it up to my shoulder as I kiss my way down, stopping again right before I reach her center. Then I take her other ankle doing the same thing. As I kiss my way down, the anticipation makes her moan. "Don't be a tease, Dante."

"Patience is a virtue, Heaven." As I reach her core, she tries moving her legs off of my shoulders. Not happening. I grip them tight, wrapping them around my head as I lean down and look up, meeting her lustrous eyes.

Then I swipe my tongue out, licking from her ass to her pussy, and making her legs squeeze me tighter. She's the sweetest thing I've ever tasted, and I want to savor every last drop.

Every ounce of self-control leaves my body as I feast on her pussy. My hands move under her dress, making it slide up as I go.

I don't stop until I can feel her soft breasts in my palms.

Rolling her nipple, I give it a pinch before moving to the other one and repeating the same motion.

Her moans grow louder with every flick of my tongue. As I move from her clit to her opening, her hands grip my hair tight, holding me in place, right where she wants me. She starts riding my face as I fuck her opening with my tongue before gliding back and giving her clit the attention it deserves. I repeat the motion over and over until she's screaming out my name and is coming so hard that her whole body is shaking.

I'm lapping up every bit of her juices as she rides out the last of her orgasm on my face. She's gasping for air, cursing, and panting my name.

Fuck, my name on her lips is the best sound I've ever heard.

I lick the last bit of her juices from my lips. Angel starts tugging me up to her, and I leave a trail of kisses as I go, only stopping to suck on each of her breasts. My head is spinning, and my cock is begging me to set it free.

"Please, Dante, I need you inside of me, now." I chuckle at her greediness.

"Anything you want, Heaven." I lift her dress over her head, tossing it to the side. She does the same with my T-shirt and gasps, getting an eyeful of my artwork.

She runs her fingers over each letter painted across my chest.

"Dante. It's beautiful. Wh...when did you do this?" Her eyes flicker up to mine. "You know this is permanent, right?"

"You were never an afterthought, Angel. You are my *only* thought. You have always been my everything. That's never going to change." I take her hand, kissing her palm softly.

She looks like she wants to say so much more but instead just closes her eyes and a single tear falls from her closed lids. She pulls me down into another kiss, one that says she understands the power she has over me.

"Mine," I growl as I move to unbuckle my pants. I kick off my boots and take off the rest of my clothes.

I stroke my cock with one hand, looking at this beautiful goddess before me. How did I get so lucky?

Lucky. Shit, he's going to murder me. Nope, now is not the time to think about the guys.

Shaking that thought from my head, I crawl up the bed until I'm staring down at her, and line myself up at her entrance. Gripping the base, I run my dick through her juices. Fuck, she's so wet for me.

"Dante, NOW," she growls impatiently at me.

My name on her lips is all it takes for me to sink my dick deep inside her.

"Holy shit, you're going to murder my pussy, D," she moans, moving her hips to adjust to my size.

"Baby, you have no idea," I say, still not moving my hips because she's strangling my dick so much. I feel like I might come any second. No, fuck that. I try to think of every possible gross thing to take my mind off of the warmth of her pussy.

Looking up at the ceiling, I need to trick my mind to stop myself from blowing my load too soon.

Glancing back down, Angel looks confused as she stares up at me. "I just needed a minute. I'm good to go now."

"Great, now move," she says, grabbing the back of my head, pulling my lips down to hers, and bucking her hips toward me.

I thrust my hips as her mouth descends on my neck, sucking, licking, and marking me everywhere she touches. Her nails claw at my arms and back, encouraging me to go harder. I take her ass in my hands, tilting her pelvis up, which gives me a whole new angle to pound into her pussy savagely.

"Dante, don't stop. Right. There. Harder," she demands.

I keep one hand gripping her ass so that I don't lose this angle and move the other between us to play with her clit. A few circles with my thumb, and she's screaming out my name again.

I keep pounding my dick into her sweet pussy as her eyes roll back in her head, her nails running down my arms, drawing blood.

"Don't tap out yet, baby. I'm not finished with you. I wanna see you ride my dick until we both come." She bites down on her lip and nods her head with pure lust blazing from her eyes.

I pull out of her, flipping her over as she lowers herself onto my thick cock. "Oh, fuck," she says breathlessly, shaking her head at me.

"C'mon, baby, take it like the rider I know you are." My girl never backs down from a challenge. She starts to ride me slowly, then picks up the pace.

I grab her hips and thrust savagely from beneath her. She looks like a queen. *My* Queen.

"Baby, I'm. Bout. To. Come. Again." Gasping for air as another orgasm explodes from her body. I feel my balls tightening, and she can hardly move. So I pound into her from below a few more times. My body shakes, and my release detonates from me, shooting cum deep into her.

She collapses on top of me, trying to catch her breath. I've never felt as good as I do right now.

A knock at the door makes both of us jump in surprise. "Angel, you in there?" Cassie says from the hallway. Angel and I burst into laughter.

"I'll take that as a yes. I'm ready whenever you are," Cassie laughs as she walks away from the door.

"I guess that's our cue," Angel says as she gets up to put her clothes on.

"Give me a minute. Just lay back down." I move to the connecting bathroom, grabbing a washcloth, and running it under warm water. Walking back into the room, I can't help but look at her in awe. *She's fucking perfect. I'm not ready for this night to end.*

I take her knees and spread them apart, running the washcloth over her center. After I've cleaned her up, I lean over, kissing her deeply.

"Alright, let's get out of here." We get dressed and head back to the party.

Cassie's leaning up against a wall, waiting as we walk back into the front room.

"So, you two made up?" All three of us laugh.

"You wanna go make up a few more times, Heaven?"

She laughs harder, pushing me away, "In your dreams, Dante."

I lean in to whisper in her ear. "Anytime, any-place."

Cassie cringes, "Eww, T.M.I. I can hear you, learn how to whisper."

Looking around the room, I see a few Sons eyeing us and whispering to each other.

I'll need to deal with that sooner than I'd like. Gabriel is going to make my life hell when he hears about this.

Chapter Seven

ANGEL

I'm ecstatic over seeing Dante again. It's been a long time since my heart has felt this full.

Ready to party with my best friends, I take Dante and Cassie's hands and lead them toward the kitchen to grab more drinks. I move over to the counter and pour us a few shots. I'm entirely too sober after the mind-blowing sex with Dante.

My body continues to ride that high, and I'm still trembling with the aftershocks from Dante having his way with me. He hit places I didn't even know existed until tonight. It was the best sex of my life, hands down.

I can only compare it to one other time, and given the circumstances, it was the best it could have been.

But this was different. This, I will feel in my bones for days.

My hand gravitates toward Dante, and I begin running my fingers across his muscular chest.

Seeing his tattoo blew my damn mind. I can't believe he tattooed *HEAVEN* on his body.

I mean, what was he thinking? Me, he was thinking about me.

He's staring at me with so much desire burning in his eyes that I consider round two.

Cassie takes off toward the front room to dance, so I walk over to let her know we are going out back to talk, just in case she needs us. Dante snakes an arm around my waist, holding me close and walking us to the backyard.

He starts nibbling at my ear and kissing my neck, letting me know exactly what he's thinking.

Untangling myself, I turn to face him as he breathes out a dramatic sigh from the loss of my touch.

"We can't fix all of our problems with sex, D. I think we need to talk and get everything out in the open. Despite my actions earlier, I can't just act like the past two years didn't happen, like you didn't just abandon me and the guys."

Dante nods in agreement. He moves to sit on a chair next to the fire pit, pulling me down with him so I'm sitting sideways on his lap.

"I'll go first. I was honest earlier and meant every word of it. I never wanted to hurt you. I was just trying to protect you, Angel."

"We covered this much," I deadpan. "You know, before the orgasms." He smirks and squeezes my thigh.

"Seriously, Angel. When Gabe realized hurting me wasn't enough to keep me away from everyone, he turned his attention toward you. At first, I thought he was bluffing, just another way for him to assert his dominance over me. Until the last night we hung out. When I got home, he was sitting at the table waiting for me. He got up, threw a handful of photos on the table, and walked away. Leaving me to process what the fuck was really going on."

"What pictures?" I ask, pulling back and watching his face under the firelight.

"They were of you in your room...sleeping. I have no idea how someone got in without you or your mom knowing, but they did. You know Gabriel has eyes and ears everywhere. Hell, he even has them inside the Reapers. You weren't safe from him, and I wasn't sure just how far he would go."

"What the hell?" I try to remember the last night we were together, but it was all so long ago the details have faded.

"When I asked him what the hell he was trying to pull, he said that none of us would ever see you again if I didn't fall in line. He said he would make you disappear if he found out I was in contact with any of you."

My body stiffens but my eyes never leave his. Gabriel is dangerous, we've all witnessed what he's capable of first hand.

"So, I did what I thought I had to do to protect you. Before you say anything, I know I should've talked to you and the guys about it, but I didn't want to risk it. He knew my weakness and wouldn't hesitate to go after you. He's a fucking psychopath, Angel."

I can't get over the thought of some creeper in my house, watching me sleep. I don't know if I feel more freaked out by the lengths Gabriel was willing to go, or that Dante kept his mouth shut about the whole thing all this time.

But *hello*, I could have been raped, kidnapped, or killed at any time by these weirdos. I think that cuts me deeper than Gabriel's psycho antics.

Dante pushes a strand of my hair behind my ear, then runs the back of his knuckles softly along my jawline.

It's always been his go-to move, and I hate the way my body immediately responds to his touch, longing for more. I lean closer to him instinctively as he takes my chin, tilting it up so that I'm looking at him. He leans forward, kissing my lips and quickly pulling back.

My head is starting to spin with everything I learned.

"Where are the guys, Heaven? They wouldn't just let you and Cassie sneak out to a party on this side of town. They're going to flip their shit when they find out." I shake out of the trance I was lost in and jump off his lap.

"I said I don't want to talk about *them*." Rage bursts from me at his mention of the guys. "I understand your reasoning behind disappearing on us, to an extent. But the fact is, you knew Gabriel sent some fucking weirdo to my house. He watched me sleep, and you said nothing. What the fuck is wrong with you? You didn't think I deserved to know this information? I don't give a fuck if you had to light the bat signal. You should have done something to give me a heads up. I should have known to be able to protect myself and my mom from your psycho-ass dad."

"I couldn't risk—"

"No. Somehow, someway, you could have warned me. I have a good idea of the shit Gabriel's involved in, and he could have easily made me disappear. You could have told literally anyone in this town and they would have let me know. All it would've taken was a snap of his fingers, and I would have been gone without a trace, D." I'm furious as I pace the yard in front of him.

"I was trying to protect you, Angel. I didn't want you living your life in fear of him. I fucked up, okay? I think about this shit daily. What I should've done differently or how I could have handled this better," Dante snaps back, pulling a handful of his own hair in frustration.

"Everyone is quick to keep me in the dark, and I'm sick of it. Why do people around me keep making decisions about me without even acknowledging what I want? It's *my* fucking life for God's sake."

"What are you talking about, Angel?"

"The guys are gone, Dante."

"What?"

"They left months ago. Pretty much the same way you did. Without a fucking word." His brows furrow, the vein in his forehead looks like it's ready to blow.

"The only difference is that Lucky has the decency to call his mom to let her know he's alive. So I guess there's that," I shrug.

"What the hell are you talking about? They left? That's absurd. They would never willingly leave you, Angel." Dante looks as confused as I feel about the whole situation.

"Willingly or not, they are gone. And I can't dwell on the choices you all make anymore. All I can do is focus on myself and try to get through each day without my chest caving in. I did my best to find them and failed. I've spent countless nights trying to figure it out, but they don't want to be found. So, I'm moving on with my life, and I don't plan on looking back."

I won't keep putting my life on hold for any of them. They made they're choices and I'm making mine.

And I won't be made to feel guilty about it.

"This has to be Gabriel's work. Otherwise, it makes no sense. Things have been worse around here the past few months. He's been keeping me in the dark when it comes to the club. My Uncle died, and I know it had some-thing to do with the Reapers, even if Gabriel didn't come right out and say it. Whenever I walk into a room, everyone gets quiet, like they don't want me to hear what's going on. He doesn't trust me and neither does the council, but I'll try to figure it all out."

"Cool, you do that. But like I said, I'm moving on. You all act as if a simple phone call is a life-or-death situation, and it's not. I'm tired of getting my heart broken by you guys. I'm over feeling like I mean nothing to you, and I'm so done living in the past. It was great seeing you, Dante. It really was, but it's time for me to go." I pull out my phone to order an Uber, but Dante pulls me into his arms, hugging me tightly.

I wish I could stay right here forever, but that's not reality anymore.

"I'm sorry, Angel. I've made a mess of things. We all have. But I'm going to make it up to you. You'll see," Dante promises.

"Yeah, well, actions speak louder than words, and you really shouldn't make promises that you can't keep. Tonight was...well, it was great and completely unexpected. I don't regret what we did because it was special to me. *You* are special to me, D. That's why I'm scared to read too much into this. Maybe it meant something to you, or maybe it didn't, only time will tell," I say, being as honest as I can.

I don't want to fall back into old habits. I have to guard my heart. Hurt me once, shame on you. Hurt me twice, well that makes me a fool, and I am nobody's fool.

"I wish I could take it all back and do things differently. I was young and dumb, and I let Gabriel use fear to manipulate the choices I made. I know it wasn't right, Heaven. Trust me when I say that I'm learning from my mistakes. I'm going to do better for you. For me. Us. So we can have a future together. Tonight meant everything to me. You need to know that. I've waited so long to finally have you in my arms. To be able to have you in my life again. Just don't give up on me yet."

I give him a hug as we head back inside to collect a very drunk Cassie, and our car arrives just as we walk back out. Cassie says goodbye to Dante and hurries into the backseat.

I hear the rumble of motorcycles coming up the street as I move to get into the car. Before I have the chance to get in, Dante pushes me up against the side of the car, taking my mouth and demanding entrance with his tongue. His kiss is fierce and rough. He's claiming my lips the same way he did my body earlier.

My mind tells me to pull away, but my body is begging for his touch. Before I can decide what I should do, he pulls away, breaking our kiss. "You need to leave, Angel. I have a good idea who's about to pull up, and you don't wanna be here for that."

"I need you to be careful, D. Don't try to be the hero, okay?"

He laughs. "A lot has changed over the past few years. I told you, I'm not the same person I used to be. I only save those worth saving now," he says with a wink as he motions for me to get in the car.

The engines roar louder as I slide into the backseat beside a passed-out Cassie. He shuts the door and turns back toward the party.

Our car passes four motorcycles on our way up the street, each rider wearing a Sons of Diablo cut. I'm glad we got out of there when we did. I'm not ready to face Gabriel just yet.

I'm awakened a few hours later by the sound of my door closing. I turn over to see if it's Mom, but it's pitch black in my room, and it takes my eyes a second to adjust. I see the tall shadow moving forward and panic rises within me. I scramble backward on my bed, backing myself into a corner. I'm reminded of Dante's words about Gabriel sending someone into my house.

The shadow reaches out to grab my arm and my fight-or-flight response kicks in. I'm careful not to yell because I don't want my mom walking in on whatever is happening here. I punch, kick, and claw at my attacker as I fight for my life.

This man is at least twice my size, if not more. He grabs me, pulling me into a bear hug, and traps my arms below his as I struggle to break free. He throws us both onto the bed and pins me down.

The panic in my chest is overwhelming, but I fight back with everything I have. I'm battling to free myself from weight of his body when all of a sudden, he leans down and licks my cheek. *Eww.*

I freeze instantly. My eyes try to search his in the dark and I see a wide smile spread across his face.

What. The. Fuck?

"I've always wondered how you might taste, a little too bitter for my taste." His words send a shiver down my spine. It's the voice of the devil.

A different kind of fear fills me. Instead, I'm painfully aware of how easy it would be to say or do the wrong thing and unleash his crazy.

"Good thing nobody asked you. Now get the fuck off me, Gabriel." I try and buck him off, which spurs him on more.

He chuckles like this is funny. "No, I don't think I will. See, you and I need to have a little conversation, sweetheart."

I freeze as my heart rate takes off, wondering what the hell Gabriel could possibly have to say to me. He laughs again, making my blood boil and every hair on my body stand on its end.

"Behave like a good little girl, or my next stop will be your mom's room."

Hell no.

I am a fighter. My mom is anything but that. She still believes in fairytales and happy endings. Me on the other hand, I've seen way too much to sit around waiting for prince charming to save me. No, I have to save myself, and right now, I need to save my mom, too.

Gabriel is more than capable of making good on his threats which has me on edge and furious at the same time. My head fills with thoughts of all the bad things he could do to my mom and I can't let that happen.

My heart pounds like the beat of a heavy drum, and the adrenaline is pumping through my veins, keeping me on high alert.

"The faster you get to talking, the faster you get out of my house," I snap at him.

He uses his thumb to pull my bottom lip out and bites it. Usually, this type of move would turn me on, but Gabriel is repulsive. Even though it looks like he doesn't age and could be on the cover of a dirty romance novel.

"Such a smart mouth on you and so feisty, but there are plenty of things to keep this mouth busy." He leans down, sniffing my hair and rubbing his nose down the side of my face.

I whip my head to the side to try to get away from him, but that just causes him to tighten his grip on me. He slides his hand down to my breast to cop a feel.

"You smell like my boy. Did he make you feel good tonight, or do I need to show you what a real man can do?"

I feel a massive bulge as he moves down my body, rolling his hips and pushing his crotch into my stomach. I try bucking him off me, but he has my arms and legs pinned to the bed. The only thing I manage to do is give him a reason to dig his nails into my skin. I'm still at his mercy.

A smile spreads across his face, and he has no right being that handsome while having such a black heart.

"You want to feel my cock stretching this tight little pussy? Or would you rather I shove it all the way down your throat?" He rubs his hard dick from my core to my stomach, and my tiny silk nightgown rides up with every move he makes, giving him easy access.

It's wrong, I shouldn't be getting turned on by his filthy mouth. But his dirty talk and good looks have something stirring low in my stomach.

I'm at war with myself, torn between doing what's right and giving in to the desire stirring inside me.

This is so fucked up.

"In your dreams. How 'bout you get the fuck off me and say what you came to say so you can leave." Squirming below him, I'm trying to keep my true feelings from bleeding into my voice.

"I have a better idea." He grabs both my wrists in one of his hands, raising and securing them above my head. He wedges his knee between my thighs and uses his free hand to spread my legs wide open so he can cram his large body into the newly opened space. This gives him a perfect view and easy access to what he wants right now. Unfortunately, it doesn't allow me to squirm out of his hold. I wiggle from his touch, trying to free one of my legs, but this fucker is strong.

Trying to keep my voice hard and low, I plead, "Gabriel, please. Don't."

"I'll make you a deal, sweetheart. If you're as dry as the Sahara, we can finish our conversation, and I'll go, but if your panties are soaking wet for me, then I'm going to see what all the fuss is about."

No matter how drool worthy he is, I can't let this happen. This is Dante's dad.

Wait. That's it.

"If I'm wet, it's your sons cum dripping out of me, not from you, you fucking psycho," I throw in his face, hoping it grosses him out enough to stop his pursuit.

"Your mouth can tell a thousand lies, but your body knows what it wants."

He moves his knee up on top of my leg to free his hand. Pushing my panties to the side, he slips a single thick finger inside me, using his thumb to circle my clit.

Do NOT react, Angel. That's what he wants.

But my pep talk doesn't stop my chest from heaving, or the flood of heat surging in my core.

"Tsk, tsk, such a bad little liar. You're dripping for me, sweetheart. Did my son not fulfill your needs?"

"Fuck you," I say breathlessly.

"Don't you worry. I'll give you what you need," he says, adding another finger and pumping in and out, stretching me wide. At this point, I'm willing my body not to enjoy a moment of this...

He pulls his fingers out and begins sucking off my juices that are covering them.

Fuck... Why is that so sexy? His touch hasn't been forceful, just commanding while waiting for my reaction. Even though my mouth says one thing, my hormones are screaming the complete opposite.

"You are sick in the head. Dante will kill you when he finds out about this. I'm young enough to be your daughter, that's disgusting."

My words are laced with venom. I'm half-heartedly hoping to strike a nerve and put a stop to this.

"My son doesn't have the guts to go against me and we both know it."

"I hope he makes it slow and painful," I breath.

"Never gonna happen."

"Fuck you, Gabe."

He pushes his fingers back into me and runs his thumb over my clit again, making it hard for me to concentrate on anything else but how good I feel. "My name sounds so sweet coming out of that pretty mouth of yours."

He curls his fingers, hitting my sweet spot, and my previous decision to deny this gets thrown right out the window. They say the line between love and hate is thin.

Well... maybe lust but definitely not love.

An orgasm hits me hard, and I bite my lip to hold back the moans rising to the surface.

"I need to taste you, sweetheart. Give me a taste, and I'll leave, I promise," he pleads. That's when I notice that his pupils are blown out.

He's fiending for more of me, like a drug addict needing their next fix. He's getting off on this, and so have I.

I've tried fighting him off, and that didn't work. I just need to get him out of my house before my mom wakes up or something worse happens. I'm about to give in when his words finally make their way to my brain.

"Your word means shit to me, Gabriel."

"You might be right about that, but I want more of you, and I'm not leaving until I get it. It would be easier if you would just concede. I want you to wrap those sexy legs around my head and strangle me with your pussy. If you do that, I'll go, and no one has to get hurt tonight."

As crazy as this sounds, I believe him. I'll do anything to keep my mom safe. Her safety comes first, even before my sanity. Fuck it... I may hate myself in the morning for this decision, but if I'm meant for hell, then I'm at least going to enjoy the ride there. Who knows, maybe my body will be his Kryptonite.

"Fine, but if I kill you in the process, then it's your fault."

"So feisty. You can try, but I'm hard to kill, sweetheart. Many have tried and failed." He chuckles, freeing my hands from his grasp. I begin rubbing my wrists where bruises are beginning to form already.

He rips my panties from my body, grabbing my hips and tilting my pelvis toward his face. "Wrap those sexy legs around me, and don't hold back. I know I won't."

He dives in, eating my pussy like a man dying of starvation. Fuuuuck... Why does this have to feel so good when I know it's so damn wrong?

I do as he demanded, wrapping my legs around his head, hopefully suffocating him, and grabbing hold of his hair, pulling as hard as I can. His grip tightens on my hips as he moans into my pussy. I'm on the verge of another orgasm, and I kinda hate myself for it.

He quickly pushes himself up, unzipping his pants. My eyes widen and I start shaking my head no. "No, Gabe, you said a taste. We agreed."

"Calm down. I'll take care of myself. But this isn't enough, and I need more. Get up," Gabe orders, smacking my ass, making me jump up. He flops down on the bed where I was lying.

"Sit on my face, sweetheart. Do all the nasty things you've ever dreamed about doing. I promise I won't tell anyone." He pushes his boxers down, freeing his cock, and oh my God, he wasn't lying about it being a monster.

It's huge, long, and thick. Did I slip into some alternate reality?

"I'm not touching that thing," I whisper while pointing at the one-eyed monster in his grip.

"I didn't ask you to, did I? Now get the fuck up here and ride my face like there's no tomorrow."

I hesitate. Before, he was playing with me, now he wants me to actively participate.

I panic about all the consequences this will bring into my life. Reluctantly, my inner bitch takes over, wondering why I should worry about others when they don't worry about me. This feels good and I'm enjoying it. So, I'm gonna take what I want, even though I wish it were anyone but Gabe here with me.

I straddle his face with my legs and lower my body to his mouth. Gabe starts twirling and flicking his tongue as I begin to move.

My body must be possessed because I start riding the fuck out of his face. Every time his nose hits my clit, I grind my pussy down harder. He moves a hand around to touch me, but I smack it away.

I want to be in charge of my pleasure. I'll be the one to take it from him however I want.

I feel the pressure building up inside of me again.

I can't hold my weight off him any longer. My legs are like jelly, allowing my weight to bear down on him as he fucks me savagely with his tongue. My orgasm explodes through my body, leaving me panting and shaking uncontrollably.

Gabe moves my hips back and forth on his face, encouraging me to move faster. He moans into me once again, and a strangled noise comes out, sounding like he's begging for one more.

I'm okay with one more since I don't want to come down from this high just yet. Plus, I'm going to hell anyway.

Too lost in all the sensations, I don't stop his hand from snaking around my body to pull on my nipples through my nightgown. He moves to my throat, turning my head slightly, so I'm watching him stroke the beast.

I slow my hips to a more seductive pace, one that matches his as my climax builds inside me.

Gabe squeezes my throat, cutting off my oxygen, but also devouring my pussy as I'm holding on for dear life. For the third time in an hour, he is the reason my body is filled with unadulterated pleasure.

As I crash back to reality, he suddenly flips us over, towering over me and stroking his cock with one hand while the other is still wrapped around my throat. He finally finds his release, shooting cum all over my naked pussy. He drops back down, lapping up the rest of the cum dripping from me.

"So delicious, sweetheart." His words pull me back to the reality of the situation. Even though my body hasn't stopped trembling from how good he made me feel yet.

He pulls off his shirt, using it to clean himself up before tossing it on top of me to wipe his cum from my body. I'm staring at his muscled chest and arms that are covered in tattoos, fighting my desire to explore each of them.

What the fuck is wrong with me? He's not a nice man. He broke into my room, but giving me three orgasms is nice, right?

"Like what you see?" He laughs as he stands to adjust his pants. "See how good a real man can make you feel?"

"Fuck you, Gabe," I roll my eyes, jumping off the bed to push him toward the door.

"Maybe next time, sweetheart. I have some-where to be right now." He chuckles, but noth-ing about this is funny.

"You got what you wanted, now go," I say, shoving him toward the door.

"Alright, I'm leaving," he laughs, tossing his hands in the air. "But first, you almost made me forget why I came here tonight. If you happen to see your boys around, tell them that I'm coming for them. And Angel, I won't stop until they're buried six feet under." I freeze, dumb-struck and at a loss for words.

"Sweet dreams, Angel. And keep calling me Gabe. I kinda like it," he whispers as he kisses my forehead and walks out.

When did I start calling him Gabe? What in the fuck is wrong with me?

I don't say another word to him. There's noth-ing left to say.

I lock the door behind him and curl up in my bed. I just let the devil himself give me three orgasms, and I gave him a nickname along the way. I can't possibly be this fucked in the head. Can I?

Later that night, I dream of a man covered in tattoos, taking me from everyone I love.

I'm standing in a room covered in blood, with bodies lying all around me. The man takes my hand and leads me away...

Chapter Eight

GABRIEL

Forcing my feet to move, I head around the corner toward my bike.

I need to leave before I change my mind. What I'd really like to do is head back in there, strip Angel bare, and sink my dick into that sweet pussy of hers. My sadistic brain can't stop from playing that fantasy on repeat. My desire rises inside me until all I can think of is her tight, delicious pussy squeezing the life out of me.

It's pure torture not to sneak back in there, push her down to her knees, and shove my cock between her plump lips.

I want to slide my dick down her throat and show her who's really in charge. The need in me burns to see her tears and spit soaking my cock as her innocent eyes beg me for more. I want to watch her choke on my dick as her rosy cheeks flame with desire. Then, when she's had more than she can handle, I want to break her for any other man.

The moment Angel watched me take my cock out, she began fighting back her inner demons. It was written all over her face.

She wanted to give in to temptation, taste, feel it stretch her pussy, feel the pleasure and the pain.

The second that I pushed my fingers into her, I wanted more. The taste of her was divine.

Angel embodies innocence, but she's begging to be set free, and I'm just the right monster to unleash her deepest fantasies.

Hopping on my bike, I take off toward the clubhouse.

Tonight was not supposed to go this way. I had a plan. Why the fuck couldn't I just stick to it?

When the prospects called, saying she was at the party with Dante, I rushed to get there. Tonight was my chance to find out what she knew. By the time I arrived, she was already gone. So, I quickly changed my plans and said fuck the consequences.

The risk of being caught in Reaper territory was high, but I needed answers, and I wasn't going to leave without them.

I don't know what came over me once I had her body trapped under my own. I had a sudden urge to taste her. So I did. It was pure instinct. The silly girl thought she could overpower me, but I quickly put her in her rightful place. Under me.

I just needed her to answer some questions about the guys. I was supposed to be in and out quickly, but the moment my cock rubbed against her, it came to life, and all my plans went out the window.

I didn't give her enough credit. She's always been mouthy, so I expected that, but I didn't anticipate her fighting back.

If it weren't for the fact she wanted to rebel against the guys, and that her better judgment had taken the night off, I wouldn't have gotten as far as I did. Maybe a part of her wanted to see if I was all talk and no action.

In some ways, she and I are the same. I understand how her beautiful mind works and all the dark thoughts that she suppresses.

There's beauty in darkness. I would know, it's where I've lived since Gloria died.

So who better to pull it out of her than me. I almost feel guilty for taking things as far as I did, almost.

Those boys probably don't even realize they've had a vixen in their midst all along. I didn't even know until tonight, but I think I've found my new obsession. The one who's fallen from grace. Maybe she can save my soul. She's the best kind of drug, and now that I've had a taste, I'm addicted to her in every way.

I wonder how long it will take her to admit to Dante what happened between the two of us. Oh, to be a fly on the wall for that conversation. He's going to flip his shit, but I wouldn't dare be the one to reveal our little secret. I seriously doubt she will say anything to him, but he will find out sooner or later. Angel will try to protect him from the truth, protect him from the big bad wolf.

Dante's so fragile. The boy wears his heart on his sleeve and cares way too much about what other people think of him. He's the complete opposite of me. The plans I had for him went out the window a long time ago.

When I first had the idea of eventually handing over the reins to him, I thought it would be easy. My plan was to bring him into the fold and mold him in my image, but he's weak.

No matter how hard I try, the kid will never be loyal to me. He could never take my throne.

His skin isn't thick enough, and he lacks the courage to be the leader the Sons need.

As soon as I took over the Sons of Diablo, I became hungry for power, and I'll stop at nothing to get it. I've made a lot of changes to the club because I'm done with barely surviving.

When I'm finished, the Sons will be the only players left in the game. This town is in for a rude awakening.

I incite fear in the prospects and demand respect from every member.

The Sons were dying when I took over, now they strongly live on. I've given them a purpose, my purpose. Nothing will interfere with what I have planned, not even my newfound obsession. No, she will play into my plans perfectly.

The day the Reapers voted King in as their new pres, shit became personal. It was probably their biggest mistake. It's been my mission to bring King to his knees for many years. Now, I'm in the position to do just that.

The need to destroy him controls my thoughts and actions more than I'd like to admit. He took everything from me, and now I'm going to return the favor. The Reapers have no idea how hard I'm going to hit them.

My history with King runs deep and the streets will run red with Reaper blood when I'm through with him and his little boys.

Yeah, I've added those boys to my hit list. They fucked up, and I will be the one to make them pay.

I created the perfect trap to get rid of them. We were going to hijack their transport, leaving them to deal with the cartel. No one wants to deal with the cartel, not even me. They are cut-throat and ruthless, even amongst their own.

I could only imagine what they would have done to King and the rest of the Reapers if my plan had succeeded.

I wasn't expecting Shadow and Sinner to be complete savages, taking out half my men by themselves. I was still holding on to hope that we could pull it off until Royal shot my older brother.

Viper was the only family that ever had my back. He wasn't the best person. He drank like a fish and bought more hookers than any man I'd ever known, but he brought me into the Sons. He helped pave my way, always supporting me, and for that, I'll seek the revenge he's owed.

Now I'm back at the drawing board and trying to regroup. I'm not above using Angel as bait to draw them out. My plan got fucked, but that just means I'll have to hit them harder next time. They think I won't touch Angel because of Dante, but they've got another thing coming.

Not only did I touch their precious Angel, but I devoured every inch of her, and I have no plans on stopping there.

I never really understood what the boys saw in her or why they constantly needed to be around her, but I see it now. She's a fucking goddess. Angel has a fighting spirit that matches my own.

She protects those she loves, even if that means selling her soul to the devil. Me being the devil, of course.

I take pride in being the monster hiding under the bed, waiting silently to destroy its prey.

I pull up to the clubhouse and head inside. Zeke, the Sons' Road Captain, is waiting for me at the door.

"Hey boss, did you get the information you were looking for?"

"Not exactly... Well, nothing useful anyway. Angel doesn't know any more than we do. The club had eyes and ears on her for months. She's been searching just as hard for them without any luck. They'll turn up eventually. They won't stay away too much longer. When they do show their faces, we will be ready for them."

Zeke nods in agreement as he moves to the bar to grab us some beers.

One of the club's hangarounds makes her way over to me. Veronica is her real name, but she goes by Roni. The woman has always been desperate for my attention.

She's been wanting me to make her my ol' lady for some years now. Been there, done that, and never going back down that road. Sorry Roni.

"You look stressed, honey. Let me help take your mind off of things for a little while," Roni begs, rubbing her hand back and forth against the crotch of my pants to get me in the mood.

"Not tonight, Roni. I'm not sure you're up for what I have in mind."

She gives me her best puppy dog eyes. "I'm always up for anything you'll give me. You should know that, baby."

Zeke hands me a beer as I catch her hand and head to one of the rooms in the back of the clubhouse. The Sons use these rooms to sleep and fuck. I can't remember the last time I took a woman back to my place for a roll in the sack. Roni doesn't know what she's in for tonight.

"You sure about this, Roni? You can say no, you know."

"I would never say no to you. Whatever you need, just let me take care of you, baby," she says, running her hands over my shoulders.

"Don't say I didn't warn you." I push her down to her knees the same way I pictured Angel. She starts unbuckling me, pulling my cock out, stroking it up and down. She's so eager for it.

She's a good-looking woman. Young, blonde, with big tits and nice curves. But she's not Angel. Throwing my head back, I close my eyes, envisioning the goddess herself on her knees before me, and I'm instantly hard as a rock.

"Open wide." I wrap my hands in her hair, pulling hard enough that she gasps. She starts swirling her tongue around the tip, then licks down to the base, getting it nice and wet.

"This will be fast and rough, baby." Her mouth widens as I slam my dick into her, hitting the back of her throat. It causes her to gag and choke. If this were Angel on her knees before me, I might have let her take control, but it isn't, so I'll close my eyes and pretend. "So hold on tight."

I'm pounding into this poor woman's mouth like a savage beast. She's got tears streaming down her face. She's half moaning and half gargling my dick right now. I look down for a second and can swear her cheeks are turning blue, but she doesn't pull back, and she doesn't try to stop. No, Roni's always up for the challenge. She deserves a medal for her deep-throat skills.

My grip tightens on her hair, and she whimpers around me, causing my balls to draw up.

"Just like that, baby. Take that dick." I moan, "Fuck!" My cum shoots down the back of her throat, and she swallows every drop, then licks me clean.

I run my hand across her jawline, almost tenderly, but not quite. "Good girl, now go grab me another beer, mine's hot."

She gets up off her knees, dusting herself off, and leans toward me as if she's about to kiss me. I quickly turn my head so that she grazes my cheek with her lips. Stalking out of the room, I pause, looking back at her. "And sweetheart, clean yourself up. The other guys might want you to take care of them later too."

She nods her head in disappointment but quickly goes into the bathroom, shutting the door behind her.

I know it's a dick move and kinda cold of me, but it's who I am. I'll never let another woman close enough to destroy me. I'll die before that happens.

Chapter Nine

ANGEL

After a restless night of vivid dreams, I stretch across my bed feeling exhausted and sore. Every few hours, I'd toss and turn in my sweat-soaked sheets, the memory of Gabriel's hands jarring me awake.

An unsettling feeling washes over me, and I can almost convince myself that it was all just a horrible steamy nightmare. I drank too much at the party, and maybe someone slipped me something heavier before I left. It's the only explanation for the shit that happened last night.

Fuck my life...

I let the devil go down on me and enjoyed every second of it. After having the best sex of my life with Dante, I let his father eat me out like I was his last meal. I must be losing my damn mind.

When Gabriel rubbed against me, it took all of my self-control to hold back the moans rising inside. I didn't want him to know how he was affecting my body and my mind. Ultimately, I failed that mission because he read my body like a book. He knew exactly what I wanted and what I needed. He gave me complete control of the situation, allowing me to ride his face and take what I wanted. I could have easily suffocated him between my thighs, but it was as if he welcomed the danger. Gabriel made my body come alive in every way possible. I can't stand how much I hate myself for giving him my pleasure.

When he left, some part of me was hoping he would come back and sink that monster cock inside of me and ruin me for good. At that moment, it felt so good to let go and just feel the things he was doing to me.

The world may perceive me as innocent, only dabbling in mischief here and there. No one sees the side of me that I keep locked away, afraid of what people might say, but it's always been there, waiting patiently to be unleashed.

Last night, Gabe unlocked the cage, and my other half was set free to run wild. I embraced the fact that I was dancing the forbidden dance. It was like breathing fresh air for the first time. I was me, and I relished in all of it.

Please don't get me wrong; it's never going to happen again. It can't ever happen again. But damn, can't a girl embrace her wild side for a little while?

I know it was wrong. Dante would kill Gabe if he ever found out that he touched me. That's why I'll take this secret to my grave. I don't need bloodshed on my hands over this, not even Gabe's.

No one can ever find out what happened between us. It would mean a war on a whole different level that I'm not willing to risk. I just hope Gabe has enough sense to keep his damn mouth shut.

My thoughts are interrupted by a knock on my bedroom door. "Hey honey, are you awake? I made breakfast for us," my mom calls out to me from the other side of the wood. I can't even imagine how different last night would have been if my mom would have walked in. I'm happy that I kept Gabe away from her, even if it meant doing the unthinkable.

"Yeah, I'm up. Give me a minute, and I'll be right there."

Glancing in the mirror at my god-awful appearance, I pull my arm up to sniff myself. Yep, I look thoroughly fucked, and smell as bad as I look. The scent is a perfect mixture of alcohol, regret, Dante, and Gabriel. Oh yeah, it's probably best to shower before my mom sees me like this.

"On second thought, I'm jumping in the shower. Go ahead and eat, Mom."

Standing in the bathroom, I stare at my naked body marked with bruises from two different men.

There are bruises along both hips from Gabe's fingers digging into them while he ravished me, and hickeys along my neck and chest from Dante worshiping me. I hesitate to get in the shower, letting the scent linger a little longer before I wash it down the drain. My conscience kicks in, telling me to stop being a whore and get my nasty ass in the shower.

Feeling like a brand-new woman after my shower, I head into the kitchen. Mom and Cassie are sitting at the table eating their breakfast and gossiping.

Cassie's mom works at the same hospital as my mom. They were best friends growing up, went to the same college and everything. Our dads were both deadbeats, leaving their families when Cassie, Lucky and I were just kids.

I was three years old when my dad left us, and only eight when he came by the house to tell us he was moving out of state. It wasn't like we cared about what he did.. The day he abandoned his family was the day he decided that being a parent was no longer his responsibility. He was only concerned with himself. He never bothered to send birthday cards or show up to anything that mattered, including my graduation. Out of sight, out of mind, I guess. He never really meant much to me, and I wasn't one of those kids whose parents divorced and they longed for them to be back together. No, my dad was a piece of shit and I knew it. Hell, the whole town knew it.

Even before he moved out of state, he was never there for us. No, everything fell on Mom's shoulders while he was out enjoying his life, partying it up. He left us with nothing, never paid child support, or helped buy clothes or school supplies. He was worthless down to his bones, and the only time he called was to weasel his way back into Mom's bed. She wasn't having that shit. She was too smart to fall for his games.

She would rather be alone than deal with his drama and messiness. It's been eleven years without having to see the scumbag's face. Good riddance.

My mom is the most hard-working person I know. She busts her ass day in and day out to ensure we have what we need, which wasn't always easy because I was a difficult child.

When I was younger, trouble called to me. The boys and I found ourselves in the worst predicaments. Let's just say the cops have shown up at our door on more than one occasion. Mom tried her best to raise me right, but we are just two different people. She had me young, so she never really got to experience life for all it's worth.

She likes laid-back, dull, and ordinary, whereas I live life a little more on the dangerous side. I let my wild and crazy run free more than she would like. I live for the thrill of the chase, being carefree, and enjoying every moment life has to offer me. Consequences be damned.

"Brenda, those flowers are beautiful. Ahh, someone's got a secret admirer." Cassie snatches the card from the bouquet, reading it out loud. *"Until next time, sweetheart."* Cassie runs up to Mom, hugging her tight.

"Does this mean you finally got some, Brenda? I swear, I thought you took a vow of celibacy or some shit. You never date, and I never see you sneaking any men out in the middle of the night. Oh, I'm so happy for you."

My mom smacks her playfully. "Those are not for me, you heathen child. They were delivered this morning, and I assumed they were either for Angel or delivered by mistake. And Cassie, can you please never mention my sex life again? You girls may be grown now, but that is a conversation that I'm not prepared to have with you just yet."

This could just be the world's most gigantic coincidence. I say a short prayer to the stars above before walking over to Cassie and snatching the card out of her hand. I read the words over and over again, letting the reality of the situation sink in.

Gabriel *fucking* Garcia just sent me flowers. My heart drops into the pit of my stomach, making me feel nauseated.

Why is this happening to me?

"Nope, they're not for me. It must have been delivered by mistake, but the flowers are pretty, so let's keep them," I say casually, tossing the card in the trash, then setting the flowers in the middle of the table.

"Hmm, okay. If you say so, honey. I thought surely they were yours. Especially considering the noises I heard coming from your room last night," Mom spouts off.

I spit my drink halfway across the room and all over the table.

Oh my God.

"Umm, that was nothing. What do you mean? What noises? Isn't it time for you to go to work, Mom?" I'm lying my ass off. Hopefully, it's believable.

"Didn't sound like *nothing* to me, but I won't pry, honey. Maybe next time, just keep it down a little." My eyes go wide. I can't believe my mom just called me out.

Curiosity burns bright in Cassie's eyes from across the table. "She may not pry, but *I* sure as hell will. Who was it? Dante, or someone else? Ahh, tell me y'all went for a round two. I was so jelly that you got it on last night. I went home to cuddle by my damn self. Ugh, you're so lucky."

"Alright, girls, that's my cue. I'm headed off to work. You girls have a good day and stay out of trouble," Mom says, kissing Cassie and me on the forehead before leaving us. Abandoning me after dropping that bomb for Cassie to hear.

Cassie dances and twerks in the middle of the kitchen as Mom closes the front door. "The spank bank needs a refill, so spill the beans, Angel."

"There's nothing to tell, so you'll have to get your refill somewhere else," I say, running off into my bedroom to get ready for work.

Cassie comes storming in. "Oh yeah, right, and I guess the whole room smells like badussy for no reason. Don't lie to me, girl. Just give me the highlight reel. Was it good or was it so bad that you now have to deny it ever happened?"

"Badussy, Cass? What the hell?"

"Yeah, badussy. Don't act like you don't know what I'm talking about. Booty, dick, and pussy, that's exactly what your room smells like. So give me the tea, woman. Don't hold back."

"Cass, just drop it, please. It was a huge mistake that'll never happen again. So I just want to forget it ever happened. I feel like a dirty whore. I don't need you judging me, too. I'm already judging myself pretty harshly right now."

"I would never judge you, but fine, keep your dirty little secrets. I'll drop it, but if you want to talk, just know that I'm always here for you, girl."

"Thanks, babe. I'm going to finish getting ready, and I'll meet you at work."

"Okay, I can take a hint. I'll see you in a few but don't beat yourself up too bad. You're only human, and we all have needs. How you fill those needs is your business. Even if it was a mistake, we all make them, especially when we're horny. And honestly Angel, it can't possibly be that bad." She gives me a soft smile before leaving.

As much as I need to talk about what happened last night, I just can't.

I want to believe Cassie wouldn't think badly of me, but even I think badly of myself and what I did.

Cassie is totally team Reapers in this war. She would shit her pants if she found out what I let Gabe do to me.

I know, I know. I didn't ask for him to sneak into my house in the middle of the night to threaten my mom, but I was no victim in the situation either, and I refuse to act like one. Enjoying what Gabe did to me was wrong, even though it felt right. Guilt floods my mind as I get ready for work.

Sitting on my bathroom counter, I apply more make-up than usual, hoping it helps cover the sin and shame lingering on me. Throwing my hair in a messy bun, I look in the mirror at the woman before me. She looks different, more brutal, and maybe even a little broken.

I've allowed the men in my life to take pieces of me until, little by little, there were big holes in my heart. Those same holes are now filled with a depthless darkness.

The damage is done, but I'm not some weak-ass woman who depends on a man for their happiness.

No, I'm a fucking fighter.

I'm loyal even to those who don't deserve my loyalty. I may be conflicted by my actions last night, but one thing is true, both Dante and Gabe set my soul on fire, lighting it in a way that I didn't know was even possible. I'm going to own that.

Straddling my Ducati, I start the engine. The rumble between my legs feels so good. Riding has always been my way of letting loose. I love everything about it. The wind blowing in my hair, excitement, speed, and danger all rolled together. There's just something about being out on the open road all by your lonesome. No particular destination. No one to tell you what to do or how fast to go. It's just you and the wind at your back.

Riding with the guys by my side or on the back of one of their bikes was fun, but I've learned over the past few months to enjoy my own company just as much.

Pulling up to Sunnyside Diner, I park and head inside. Work is always fun. Cassie and I make everything into a competition. Who can get orders out the fastest, who can take the most tables, who can make the most tips. Whatever we can think of to make the day go by quickly.

We also secretly crack jokes at the expense of our customers for most of the shift.

The non-tippers, the grumpy old men, and the snobby wives become the butt of most of them. We get through our shift without her bringing up my mystery man, and I'm grateful for that.

By the time our shift is over, the moon is resting high in the sky, and Cassie asks if I want to go out with her again tonight.

"I think I had enough excitement last night, Cass."

"Fine. Party pooper." We walk outside the diner to see Shadow and Dante standing toe to toe. I rush over, trying to put myself between them.

"What the fuck is going on?" I ask both of the men. Shadow looks like he's ready for a fight, and Dante isn't backing down.

"I stopped by to see if you wanted to go for a ride after your shift when Shadow showed up."

"Okay, then why do you look like you're ready to tear each other apart?" I inquire, wedging myself between the men.

Shadow snaps out of the staring contest to finally look down at me. "Lucky sent me to check up on Cassie." So he cares enough to send someone to look after Cass but not me? That stings a little.

He strolls up to Cassie, taking her hand and leading her to his bike. There are no words exchanged between them, but she looks oddly comforted by his actions.

"Your boyfriend needs to find his way back to the other side of town before he lands himself in a whole mess of trouble," Shadow says as he pulls Cassie onto his bike to leave.

Dante just shrugs. "I'll take my chances, but thanks for the warning."

"It's your funeral, kid," Shadow says, taking off with Cassie, leaving me alone with Dante. I wasn't prepared to see him so soon. My skin feels like it's shrinking, becoming too tight from the anxiety taking over me.

"You could have called, you know."

Dante puts his hands in pockets, looking down at the ground. "Wow, don't act so happy to see me, Heaven." "I'm sorry, D. I didn't mean it like that. But it's not safe for you to be here. The clubs are in the middle of a war, and you show up in Reaper territory to go for a ride?" I explain, trying to backtrack on the bitchiness in my tone.

"Well, I just needed to see you again, and I didn't particularly like the way we left things last night. It just felt unfinished, leaving everything hanging in the air. Besides, I'm finished living my life in fear of what ifs, Heaven. For two years, that's all I've done. I'm over it. I'm going to start living the way I want, and that starts by having you back in my life. So do you wanna go for a ride with me or not?"

I walk up to him, wrapping my arms around his neck, pulling him down to my mouth. I'm so happy that Dante is taking his life back and not allowing Gabe to control him any longer. It may be a long hard road, but this is something he needs to do for himself. I've waited years for him to make this decision.

Dante doesn't need any more encouragement from me.

His tongue glides across my lips, demanding entrance. The moment I open for him, his tongue sweeps in. He grabs my ass, lifting me in the air. Instinctively, my legs wrap around his waist, clinging to him like a spider monkey. The passersby are getting one hell of a show from us right now.

We are basically dry humping for the world to see in the middle of the sidewalk.

I pull away, breaking our kiss. "I'd love to ride you, D. I mean go for a ride with you."

Someone clears their throat behind me, and Dante looks up in shock. He drops my legs to the ground in a swift move, making me stumble to catch my balance.

"What the hell, D?" I spin around to get a look at what he's staring at and find three familiar assholes staring back at me.

Chapter Ten

ANGEL

Fuck me, could this day be any more complicated? I mean, seriously, they pick today of all days to show back up. The men in my life just keep fucking with me.

My heart beats erratically as if it will explode at any given second. When did they get back? Why are they here now? So many unanswered questions float through my mind, but I can't get my mouth to form a sentence. I can barely contain the anger flooding through my veins at the moment. The three of them look equally upset by what they just witnessed, but that's not my concern.

Lucky is the first one to speak. "So, when did this happen?"

Stepping forward and waving his arms between Dante and me. Confusion and hurt are written all over his face, but he doesn't get to look hurt when he's the one who left me.

Dante takes a step toward them. "Look," he starts, but I slam my hand to his chest, pushing him back.

"No, don't you dare try and explain anything to them, Dante."

Dante takes me by the shoulder, pulling me into his embrace. He slowly rubs his hands along my arms, trying to calm me. He leans down, placing his forehead against mine. "Heaven, just hear them out. Please, baby, I know you're upset, but they're here now. Isn't that what you wanted?" He gently places a kiss on my lips, then pulls back, giving me some space. I guess he doesn't care too much about the guys' opinion on the matter either.

Briefly thinking over Dante's plea, I take a deep breath and exhale before turning to face the guys. My heart is torn. On one hand, I'm relieved and happy they are here and safe. On the other hand, I can't keep doing this. If I give in now, then I'm only allowing them to think this is acceptable. It's not.

I'm sick and fucking tired of everyone playing games with my heart.

"Get out of your head, Princess," Royal says so nonchalantly that it makes my blood boil and I see red.

"You think it's that easy, huh? You know what? Fuck you. Fuck all of you. I don't need this shit," I proclaim as I move to straddle my bike and get the hell out of dodge.

"Kick our ass, curse us, do what you need to do. Just get on with it already," Royal yells out to me.

My body trembles as I grab my helmet, placing it on my head. "What do you want me to say? That I hate you? That I'm hurt? I've thought about how this conversation would play out countless times over the past three months, but now that you're here, I have nothing to say. I just know I don't want to be anywhere around you." I'm as honest as I can be with him. Does it even matter anymore why they left? They made their decision, now they have to live with the consequences and stay the fuck away from me.

Stalking up to me, Jaxon grabs a hold of my wrist before I can take off, his fingers burning my flesh with his touch. "I need to know... Is it Dante, then? Is that who you choose?" he asks.

"No, Jax, I choose ME. You left me alone to fend for myself, and guess what? That's exactly what I did. I learned how to live without all of you. So don't expect me to welcome you back with open arms." I shake my head in disbelief.

"You think I had a choice in the matter? Do you think any of us did?" Jax yells in my face, and I hop off my bike so fast, shoving him hard.

"Who the fuck do you think you are, yelling at me like that?"

Jaxon viciously pulls my body into him, grabbing my hair and pulling my head back. His mouth is directly over my ear as he whispers, "Do you need a reminder, Trouble? Because I'd be happy to give you one."

This has gone on long enough. They have no remorse, and clearly they think this shit's funny. It's my life they're fucking with, and I'm putting a stop to it right now.

I push Jaxon back toward the guys. "Let me take a guess. Daddy King made you do it." I look between them, needing them to hear me loud and clear. "First, Gabe made you leave," pointing at Dante. "Then King did the same with y'all, right?" All three of their heads nod in agreement.

Wow, I just can't believe this shit.

"Angel, we—" Lucky starts, stepping forward as I take a step back.

"No, save it. You are all pitiful. Weak. You're all grown-ass men taking orders from another man. Does he wipe your ass for you too? I thought our bond was stronger than that. You're nothing more than pawns for these men to play with, and you allowed them to break us."

"We were trying to protect you," Royal yells.

"Keep telling yourself that if it makes you feel better, Royal. Is that the bullshit King fed you to get you to fall in line? That you were doing this for my benefit? You know how devastated I was when Dante left..."

"This was different." Royal looks at Dante for a moment and back to me.

"You three did the same fucking thing, no difference." I stare at Royal, giving him every ounce of anger I've swallowed back for the last three months. "Jax was attacked the night before you took off, and for a solid week, I thought you guys were laying in a ditch somewhere. Not one of you thought to pick up a phone and let me know that you were okay. I had to find out through Cassie that you were even alive. You let my mind wander into the darkest places while I searched for you, but the worst part is knowing you left me by choice.

"Why the fuck aren't you hearing us? It was a choice made to keep you safe. How was it even a choice at all?" Lucky pleads.

"It was a decision each of you made willingly. Do you know what that does to a person? Do you have any idea of the hell you put me through? Making me doubt everything between us. No, you don't have a clue because I would've never done those things to you. Hell, I would've gone to war for any of you. But you all just walked away without a word. I thought I was your Heaven, your Princess, and your Trouble, but in reality, I wasn't any of those things. I was nothing. You four won't define who I am any longer, and I refuse to let my happiness live and die with you. I've found my way in your absence and I'm doing just fine on my own now. It took me a while to get here, but I'll do whatever it takes to protect my sense of peace. So please, just stay away from me. You owe me that much."

I get back on my bike and take off before they have a chance to respond. I can hear them yelling out to me as I ride off, but I can't make out what they're shouting, and right now, I don't care.

I was able to say what I needed without interruption. They played me for a fool one time too many. Now that it's off my chest, it feels like a weight has been lifted from me.

I know I will have to deal with this eventually, but right now, it's too fresh. I meant what I said. They are weak. Weak-ass little boys letting another man decide their fate. I would never allow anyone to come between us. Even though I'm not sure there is an us to come between anymore.

Hitting the open road, I ride for hours along the coast to clear my mind. So much has gone down in the past twenty-four hours that I feel like my brain will combust soon. The past three months have been a whirlwind for sure, but everything that's happened since last night feels like a tornado that's trying to take me out for real. I'm not sure how much more I can stand without completely breaking down. It's just too much for one person to have to deal with on their own.

The perfect view becomes clear as I pull over at my favorite spot on the beach. It's peaceful out here. Breathing in the salty air, with the moon hanging low over the ocean and the crashing waves making music for my soul.

I dismount my bike to get closer to the water.

Walking along the beach brings back so many good memories of me and the guys.

We've spent so much time out here together that it's hard not to think of them. But one memory in particular latches on to me.

Our moms are laying in the sand sunbathing. Cassie is splashing in the ocean while Lucky and I are building sandcastles. We just finished building a moat around our castle to keep it from being invaded when Lucky takes my hand in his, tugging me toward him.

"Angel, promise you'll be mine forever, and I will build you a castle just like this one when we get older. The castle and I will keep you safe."

"You don't have to build me a castle, Luck, I'm already yours."

"Forever?" he asks, looking worried about my answer.

"I pinky swear, Luck. You and me, forever." I hold out my pinky and he takes it with his own. We seal our promise to one another by kissing our knuckles while our pinkies are locked together.

Before Lucky disappeared, I would have kept that promise to him forever. But keeping it now means opening myself up to the possibility of being hurt again, and I just don't think I can do that to myself. I thought I was ready to forgive

Dante, but seeing the guys brought the pain of him abandoning me back to the surface.

I sit down and dig my feet in the sand. There's no better feeling than letting yourself become one with the earth. Well, okay, maybe I can think of one or two other things that feel better. Like Gabriel's tongue or Dante's dick being buried deep inside me. Other than that, there's no better feeling.

Laying back, I look up at the stars and name as many constellations as I can see. I've always had a slight obsession with the stars and the moon. It's all so fascinating to me and also makes me realize how minuscule I am in the grand scheme of things.

Someone or something created all of this, the whole universe, but also took the time to make me beautifully imperfect. It's one of the reasons I've always lived life the way I have. I want to enjoy every second of this unpredictable life A meteor could fall down from the sky and crush me this instant.

This only reminds me that if that did happen, then the relationships I spent my entire life nurturing will be gone forever.

"Hey," Jaxon calls out to me, disturbing my deep thoughts. He slowly walks up, nervously taking a seat beside me in the sand.

"Hey." Most of the anger that I felt earlier has subsided, leaving me with only hurt and abandonment. Two things I've spent the last three months trying to avoid, but I can't deny them right now when they are so present inside me.

"I know you're mad and need space, but can we talk? Please, Angel. I've been going insane without you."

The knot stuck in my throat grows tighter. I'm holding back the tears burning my eyes. There's no way I can speak without showing him how upset I am by just the sound of his voice.

Instead of speaking, I nod my head. Jaxon never calls me by my name. It's always Trouble, baby, or whatever other nickname he comes up with. Him calling me by my name means he's serious. It's a side of Jaxon I rarely get to see unless he's mad.

He's burning a hole in the side of my face with his glare. I'm forcing myself to hear him out right now, even though everything in me says to cut and run. I need this for my sanity as much as he probably needs it for his, too.

"I'm listening, Jaxon. Say what you need to say, then leave me to the stars. We were right in the middle of a deep conversation before you so rudely interrupted."

Jax chuckles and gives me a smirk. He knows far too well nothing interrupts me and my conversations with the sky.

Jaxon starts telling me all about what happened after they dropped me off that night. He tells me about how Gabriel set them up. The fire, the war, the death, and everything in between. He finishes by telling me how King forced them to leave when Royal shot Viper.

I sit, quietly listening to his story. I'd rather he get it all out than interrupt him with my questions. I'm still not sure how I feel about everything, but then he goes on to tell me how Shadow and Sinner had to babysit them and physically restrain him to keep him from coming home to me.

King destroyed all their phones before they left, and they were taken to one of the club's safe houses. Jax says Shadow broke a few of his ribs when he tried to leave. King was apparently trying to keep the guys safe from Gabriel, who just happens to be on a warpath. Gabriel's parting words from last night replay over and over in my head.

After a week had passed, King sent them all to the Reapers of Havocs San Diego chapter, and that's where they have been ever since. My heart hurts thinking about all they went through that night. My mind is spinning, and I don't understand why King couldn't have just told me all of this when I showed up at the clubhouse that day. It would've saved me from a lot of heartache and feeling so betrayed by all of them. Did he think I wouldn't understand or that I didn't deserve to know?

Jax goes on to say that one of King's spies inside the Sons of Diablo MC told them that Gabriel had eyes on me at all times and somehow he had someone tap into my phone to monitor my communications so he would know if I had contact with them.

Although I'm not completely shocked considering the guy crept his way into my bedroom last night.

King told them it would be unsafe for the guys to contact me. That he was scared that Gabriel would stop at nothing to get to Royal and he would use his greatest weakness to do it. *Me.*

The guys left the San Diego chapter against King's wishes and now he is furious with them. They'd assumed Gabriel had calmed down enough to where they could come back and figure out a plan. Jax says they couldn't stay away forever, and they needed to make a game plan to get back to their lives, and more importantly, to me.

After understanding everything that happened on their side, everything they went through, I have a little more empathy about the situation. Not that it makes me instantly feel better or want to forgive them, but at least now I know.

"I can tell by the look on your face that you're still processing everything. I'll do whatever it takes to make things better between us, Angel."

"I know, Jax. I know. I still don't completely understand why you guys didn't find a way to get in contact with me. I realize now that the phones were tapped, and that wasn't an option. But why couldn't you have snail mailed something to me or make someone in the club pass along a message... Something."

"We tried, Trouble. We really did. For weeks we begged anyone and everyone to let you know we were okay, to tell you that we would come back as soon as possible. King wasn't having it. Apparently, he put out a gag order on our whereabouts until further notice. No one was willing to go against his orders for us. The best we could do was a single call to Lucky's mom, but even then, King was listening to make sure no one slipped up and said anything.

"None of this makes sense, Jax. He's known me my whole life. Why didn't he trust me enough to tell me what was going on? He can use that lame-ass excuse about keeping me safe all he wants, but I call bullshit on that one. He had ulterior motives. I'm sure of it."

I'm not in the right headspace to continue or have any more deep conversations today. I should probably tell the guys about Gabriel's threat, but I need to find a way that won't involve them digging further than the warning I was given.

Jax leans over, kissing me on the forehead. "I'll give you the space you need for now, but I'm not giving up on us. I'll prove to you that I'm the man who deserves to be by your side."

"It feels like an eternity has passed since we were in that place, Mischief. I know we left things unfinished when you left, but I'm not sure we can get back there. Not with all the damage separating us."

"Maybe, or maybe Dante has more to do with it than you're willing to admit. Either way, I'm still the best man for you. Like I said, I'll prove it. Just wait and see." He gets up, dusting the sand off him.

"Goodnight, Trouble. I'm back now and the devil himself can't keep me away from you."

Chapter Eleven

ANGEL

Sunnyside Diner is extremely slow for a Saturday afternoon. This week has gone by way too fast, but my shift is dragging on. Our boss, Morgan, sent Cassie home early after the morning rush. Since Cassie left, I've spent most of my shift daydreaming or lost in thought. I've been thinking about life, divine fate, and all that jazz.

The guys and I ended up here somehow, but was it an act of fate or just dumb decision-making on their part?

Life is unpredictable, constantly changing and pushing us to adapt. I always try to live in the present and enjoy life as it comes, take the good with the bad and try my best to stay positive through it all.

Sometimes that's easier said than done. The universe is a moody bitch. Depending on how she wants to treat you at any given moment, you can go from experiencing the best moments of your life to the worst in the blink of an eye. From overwhelming joy to the most excruciating pain you've ever felt before in an instant.

The strongest people that I know are the ones who didn't let the universe break them. When the easy choice would have been to quit or give up, they took their pain and turned it into motivation and strength to keep pushing forward like warriors.

I've spent the past week thinking about Jax's words to me when we were on the beach. I can't see myself just accepting the boys back knowing we could be in the same situation as soon as Gabriel finds out that they are back in town.

Considering his stalker ways, I'm surprised he hasn't figured it out yet. Maybe he's just biding time, waiting to make his next move, but I'm not waiting for the other shoe to drop. I'm going to fight to take control of my life. I'm not going to let any of these assholes dictate my future any longer.

I've been thinking about different ways to get them out from under this shit. Most of the ideas I come up with are risky as hell and the guys wouldn't approve. I just need to think of something that is soundproof. Something that won't fail and won't put me behind bars.

The guys have respected my wishes. Giving me the space I asked them for. Well, that's not completely true. Cassie went out and got us all new phones when she heard about Gabriel monitoring my calls.

So they have all been texting me daily from their new phones to see if they are out of the doghouse yet, and the answer is still no. At least, not until I can find a way for us to not end up exactly where we are now. Then, and only then, can we try to make our way back to how things used to be. They haven't shown up unexpectedly, so I guess they get points for that.

I'm wiping down tables when I hear the front door chime with an incoming customer. I put the towel I was using away and grab some menus. When I look up across the counter, I see three Sons of Diablos heading for a booth in the corner. I try to keep my panic to a minimum and just act normal, as if they were any other customer.

Sunnyside is in the Reapers territory, but it's close enough to the border that sometimes we randomly have Sons that come in to eat. It's rare, but not unheard of. So I keep that in mind as I take the menus to their table. I notice two of them are wearing prospect cuts, so they aren't patched in just yet.

"What can I get you fellas to drink?" I ask them, trying to sound calm and casual.

They order a round of coffee and water. I move behind the counter to prepare their drinks, wondering if I should let the guys know about this. Since they are still supposed to be in hiding, I decide that it's not a good idea and it's best not to say anything unless I need to involve them.

I know they would all rush down here to play Captain Save-A-Ho if I called them, and we don't need that heat on us. We need to be prepared before they show their faces around town again.

I place their drinks on the table and ask, "Are you boys ready to order?"

The only patched Son chuckles while staring at my name tag. "Angel, is it? Well, Angel, I don't see any boys around here," he says while grabbing his crotch and leaning back in the booth for me to see the disgusting act.

"If you say so. Are you ready to order or not? I have other customers to check on." Now, they all laugh in a way that creeps me out.

"You're the Reapers' girl, right?" One of the prospects asks while looking my body up and down like he wants to bend me over the table and fuck me with his tiny micro penis.

"The fuck? No, I'm not, and who the fuck are you? Asking me twenty questions like you know me. I don't know you from Adam. If you think I'm about to sit here and play these little games with you, you've got another thing coming."

"Gabriel said you had a smart mouth on you, little girl. I guess he wasn't lying. Look, we don't want any trouble."

My spine straightens at the sound of his name, and I cut him off before he can continue with whatever he's saying.

"Do I look like someone who gives two flying fucks what Gabriel says about me? Do you want to order food? If not, I'll leave you to finish your coffee."

"We'll just have our coffee, thanks," the other prospect states as I turn to walk away. "Oh and, Angel, Gabriel wanted us to relay a message to your little boyfriends." Walking toward the counter, I look over my shoulder to see all three of them standing up and drawing their guns.

A quick reaction has me diving behind the counter, yelling out to everyone to get down just before the bullets start flying. The customers are screaming in panic. These idiots think they are big, scary men with their guns, and Texas-sized egos. I can't be bullied, not by them and sure as fuck not by Gabriel.

On the ground, I army crawl, making my way to the back of the diner. I tell everyone in the kitchen to call the police as I get up off the ground into a crouched position. *Shit!* My phone is still behind the counter, and I can't get to it without being seen.

There's an emergency exit in the back of the diner, and after checking my surroundings, I decide to make a run for it. I rise from my crouched position and run like the wind, busting through the back door and colliding with a mass of solid muscle covered in tattoos.

"Going somewhere, sweetheart?"

With the adrenaline still coursing through me, I look up, dazed and confused, after smacking into the brick wall in front of me.

"What the fuck, Gabriel? You really have no conscience, do you? Putting innocent lives at risk like that."

He runs his hand down the side of my face, making goosebumps pop up all over my body. He leans down, taking a big whiff of my hair and then burrowing his nose into my neck. I'm stiff as a board, holding completely still while my heart beats frantically. I have no idea what this man is about to do. He is so unpredictable.

The warmth of his breath on my skin sends chills down my spine. I can't stop my body from shuddering at his close proximity.

"What do you want, Gabe?" The words come out as barely a whisper, with no power behind them.

"You," he proclaims, making my pussy clench. He should not have this effect on my body. I should not wish for him to lean in just half an inch closer to feel his mouth on my skin once more.

"You just had your boys shoot up my place of employment because you wanted me? That's hard to believe, and a horrible tactic if you ask me."

He brushes his nose along my neck then swipes his tongue out, getting a taste.

He grabs me forcefully by the hair, angling my head so that he has better access to my neck. I can't help the moan that escapes me as he begins to suck and bite my neck like a fucking vampire. He still has a firm grip on my hair when he pulls back. "I wanted to test you. I needed to see if you would go running back to your boys when shit went down, and you didn't, did you? You ran, but you never called them for back-up when my boys showed up. That says a lot to me."

"That doesn't mean shit, Gabe. All that means is when my fight-or-flight kicked in, I chose flight versus being shot to death. This wasn't some act of loyalty toward you, so don't make it out to be that in your head."

"You're right. You aren't loyal to me, but you are loyal to yourself, and that's all I need to know. I gotta go, but I'll see you soon, sweetheart. Very soon."

As Gabe backs away from me, it's like the bubble around us popped. My senses start to come back, and I can finally focus on everything around me. The sirens are getting louder as Gabe takes off from the diner on his motorcycle. Shaking my head and trying to clear the fog from my brain because... What. Just. Happened. Why does he want to test me? And how the fuck is shooting up the diner a damn test? Something is mentally wrong with him.

I push myself off the wall and move to check on everyone inside. I'm praying they're alright.

As I reach for the door handle, someone grabs my arm from behind, stopping me from opening the door.

"Care to explain what that was all about?"

Lucky grabs my wrist, spinning me around to face him. *Shit!*

"Not particularly, no. The diner was just shot up by the Sons, and I need to go check on everyone, not sit out here and gossip with you, Ponyboy."

"Fuck that, the diner was shot up and what? You were out here behind the building making out with the guy who set the whole thing into motion. What the fuck has gotten into you, Angel?"

I yank my arm from his grasp and poke him in the chest with my finger. "First of all, asshat, there was no making out going on. Second, if there was, how is that any of your fucking business?"

"Does Dante know you're making out with his *dad*? That's disgusting Angel."

"Are you fucking kidding me right now? There was no making out. I'm not going to discuss this right now when people could be in there bleeding out for all we know." I reach for the door and Lucky slaps my hand away, pulling it open for me.

"We are going in here to check on everyone, then you and I are going somewhere to talk," Lucky demands.

I nod my head, not being able to stand the look of disappointment on his face right now. He looks like I just killed his puppy and that's not okay with me.

We head inside through the alley door, checking on the workers in the back first. Everyone is shaken up but seems to be okay. We talk to each of the employees in the back before moving on to the dining area.

The windows are shattered, broken glass is everywhere, but everyone seems to be fine. You know, other than the mental aspect of being inside an establishment while it's getting shot up over a turf war in their hometown. I mean, they still have to deal with that, but no one is physically hurt, so that's good.

It looks like it was just a scare tactic. The customers say they were pointing their guns in the air or at the windows to cause damage but not intentionally trying to hurt someone.

Hmm. Maybe the devil does have a conscience after all.

The cops have a few questions for me that I answer briefly, but decide to leave out a few small details, like the fact that it was the Sons and Gabe who did this.

Gabe has plenty of people on the police force working for him. I don't want to be labeled as a rat only for them to get away with this. It's not beneficial for anyone involved.

Lucky takes my arm and leads me away from all the commotion. "What are you doing, Luck? I'm exhausted. I need to go home, shower and sleep for at least three days."

"Wonderful, Princess, but first we need to talk about what happened back there. So, let's go." He hands me my phone and keys, which he must have grabbed from inside while I was being questioned. "Please don't fight me on this, Angel. Meet me at the clubhouse. I have to get my bike. It's parked on the side street behind the building."

"Fine, but only because you look like someone stole your favorite Power Ranger and snapped the head off of it."

"This feels worse than that, Angel. Way worse."

Well, great, now I feel worse than I already did.

Chapter Twelve

ANGEL

I'm feeling nervous as hell about having this discussion with Lucky. I need to figure out what to say because if anyone can tell that I'm lying, it's Lucky. He reads me like a book and knows all my tells.

I pull into the clubhouse and park next to Royal's bike.

Just great, that means we will have an audience for this. Now would probably be a good time for me to just run away and hide.

Lucky pulls in beside me, jumps off his bike, storming over to me.

"What the fuck are you thinking, Angel? Letting Gabriel fuck with you like that. Have you lost your damn mind?"

"You have no right, and no idea the shit I've been through. So check that shit at the door before you start running your mouth." I remove my helmet and hop off my bike to get in his face.

"I have every right to be concerned. Just because I fucked up one time—" he starts, but the daggers I'm shooting his way have him backtracking.

"Okay, fine, one *major* time. It doesn't take away from the years I've been by your side. Since when did we start keeping shit from each other? Maybe you're right, I don't know what you went through, but that works both ways. Why don't you start fucking explaining, so I can better understand? Because this looks hella bad from where I'm standing." He crosses his arms, scolding me once again.

"Oh, I don't know, Luck, maybe around the same time that you became Casper and ghosted me. I couldn't really tell you my secrets when I don't know where the fuck you are, could I?"

"Whatever." He rolls his eyes. "I guess I deserve that. That still doesn't explain why the fuck Gabriel felt so comfortable getting all up in your space the way he did. Was he sucking on your neck? That's fucking disgusting. You know that, right?" Luck starts being dramatic, acting like he's going to throw up.

"It's not like I asked him to be all over me. Newsflash, asshole, Gabriel does whatever the fuck Gabriel wants to do. This isn't something new. He just shot up the diner for God's sake, and you think I can stop him from being in my space? And he may or may not have licked my neck a little, I can't say for sure. I was traumatized, incoherent, and possibly delusional. I control him about as much as anyone else in this town does."

Lucky looks at me sideways. Maybe I have lost my mind. Who fucking cares? We have bigger fish to fry.

"Traumatized? You? The girl who runs toward the flames instead of away like every rational human being on this earth?" He rolls his eyes and continues to call me out.

"You really expect me to believe that shit? Who are you trying to fool, sugar lips, me or yourself? I saw the way you reacted to him. I'm not blind. You fucking wanted him. Not once did you push him away or tell him to back the hell off."

I pushed him off, *didn't I*? Oops, I don't think I did. I'm so fucked in the head.

"I don't really see why I have to explain myself to you. Are you concerned about my well-being or are you just jealous?"

"Jealous? You're kidding me, right? Why the fuck would I be jealous of Gabriel? It's not jealousy, it's concern, and I'm a bit creeped out if we're being honest. Why would you let that scumbag anywhere near you?"

"Well, thanks for your concern. Are we done?"

I need to get the hell out of here before I spill the beans. He knows I'm lying. I might as well have "guilty" written across my forehead because he ain't fallin' for my bullshit. Hell, I'm not even falling for my bullshit.

New plan, nod more and say less.

"What the fuck? No, we're not done."

"Okay, calm your britches. It was just a question. Don't get your panties in a twist."

"I don't wear panties, you know that. Free ballin' all day, baby. So cut the shit and spill it." He swirls his hips, shaking his junk at me. "Just tell me what's going on, Angel, or else."

"Or else what? What you gon' do, Luck?" I spit, crowding his space so he has to look down. Our lips are almost touching.

I'm not scared of Lucky. At the end of the day, he's my Ace, my partner in crime, my ride or die. He may want answers, but he still loves me no matter what.

"I'll call up the guys and we can have a group discussion about this, then you can explain to Dante why you let his dad put his dirty, greasy-ass paws all over you."

Okay, maybe he's not my Ace. I take that shit back.

"You wouldn't dare. Snitches get Stitches, Luck. Is that what you want?" I challenge him, pushing his ass away from me.

"Oh I would, just try me. Get to talking or I'm making that call. Then you can explain yourself to all of us. It's your choice. What's it gonna be, Trouble?"

"Oh, so we're tattling now? You think you know a person. Don't threaten me. I don't owe you guys shit. You left and I did what I had to do to make it through. You don't get to judge me for that, none of you do. I won't stand here and listen to it. You guys put me through hell, and I thought I lost you forever."

"So what? We left and you crawled into bed with the devil thinking we wouldn't mind because we weren't there to see it? Seems sketchy to me. And how long are you going to use the 'we left you' thing as an excuse to do fucked-up shit? I just need to know a timeline to prepare myself."

"As long as I fucking want, asshole. I didn't crawl into bed with him. Maybe he crawled into bed with me. Have you thought about that?" I spit, tapping my finger against the side of my head, being overly dramatic.

"Wow. I don't even know who you are right now. He's the reason we had to go into hiding. He's the reason we've been at war for the past few years. The dead bodies in the streets? That's all because of him."

Our playful banter is gone and the seriousness hits me hard.

"I know that, Lucky. I'm not stupid. I know exactly who he is and what he's capable of. On the other hand, your actions are pretty questionable these days, so—"

The door slams to the clubhouse, drawing my attention away from Lucky. King comes out looking pissed and heading straight for us.

"What the hell are you two yelling about out here?" He turns, spitting his venom at me. "And didn't I tell you to stay the hell away from here? What's the matter? You don't know how to listen, girl?"

Lucky moves, placing himself between me and King.

"Sorry about that, King, we'll keep it down," Lucky says, trying to calm him.

"I told her to stay the hell away from here and apparently she has a problem following simple instructions."

"Wait. You banned her from the clubhouse? Why would you do that? She's family. No different than the rest of us."

"Oh, there's a big difference. Did you make her your ol' lady and not tell us? I don't see her wearing a ring on that little finger of hers, or a Reapers patch. So unless I'm mistaken, she's no family of mine. What you do outside of here is your business. Inside these walls? That's mine, and I don't wanna see her around here again."

"That's not fair, King. We just spent three months away from her and this is the only place we are safe right now," Lucky tries, pleading with him.

"Clearly, three months wasn't long enough to keep the trash away."

The door to the clubhouse opens once more, allowing Royal and Sinner to walk out. They immediately stop to watch everything unfolding with confusion written across their faces. I've had about all the third-degree questions that I can take. Enough is enough. I move around Lucky getting in King's space.

"Trash? Wow, you have some nerve. This is all your fucking fault, anyway. They left me on your orders, and instead of you doing the right thing and telling me what was going on, you decided to keep it a secret. You left me in the dark when you didn't have to. You basically held them hostage for three months. You kept them from their families. From me. Over your fucking war. They deserve better than that and better than you. I've always thought of you as a father figure, but you're no different than Gabriel. All this club shit is tearing this town apart, but do you try to find a way to make peace between the clubs? No, you just keep it going or add to it."

King strikes me across the face, back handing me so quickly that I don't even have time to process what's happening.

I go down.

Hard.

Lucky tries to break my fall but comes up short.

Royal takes off running toward his dad, throwing a punch which lands solidly along King's jaw. It catches him off guard and makes him stumble.

Royal doesn't stop there. He attacks King, swinging his vicious, heavy fists at his father's body and face. And King, he isn't just taking it. No, father and son are in an all-out brawl outside the clubhouse.

The other Reapers and a few hangarounds spill out from inside to see what all the ruckus is about. Sinner is trying to get between Royal and King with no luck. Royal is fighting his dad like a savage madman, defending my honor.

Royal knocks King down to the ground and jumps on top, pounding his face in with each blow. Both men are covered in blood as they continue to fight. King is trying to buck Royal off of him while taking shots at his kidneys, as if that would help him. Royal is in beast mode. Which is unfortunate for King because not too many people can match his strength and agility in a fight.

Shadow makes his way outside and runs over to help Sinner, who is the only person crazy enough to try and break them up. Shadow hauls Royal off of King like he weighs nothing. He wraps him up on the ground in what looks like a wrestling move to keep him from attacking King. Sinner moves over to check on King, who is still laying on the ground bleeding.

At some point during all this, I didn't notice that Lucky had pulled me into his arms and is now holding me tight, almost possessively.

After a moment, Royal seems to have calmed down, so Shadow releases him. They both stand and Royal looks from me to his dad.

He walks over to King and kicks the shit out of him one last time. No one tries to stop him. Everyone is just staring with their mouths hanging half open at what they just witnessed.

"You ever lay your hands on her again, and I'll be the one to put you in the ground, old man." Royal spits on the ground next to King's head in pure disrespect.

He walks over to me and Lucky on the ground. "Get her out of here. I'll bring her bike by the house and drop it off. She doesn't need to be here for this."

Lucky nods his head while I just sit there, speechless. He kisses me on the cheek and rises, offering me his hand to help me get up. King's hit must have left me a little more dazed than I realized because once I'm standing, I stumble. I almost fall back down, but Royal pulls me into his arms, holding me up.

"Fuck, never mind, she can't ride like this, Luck. She'll end up getting hurt."

Shadow walks over, handing Royal his keys. "Just take my truck, brother. Make sure she gets home safe."

I wasn't expecting that kind of response from Shadow, not that I know him very well, but still, I disrespected his pres, which set everything in motion. I thought he would be pissed over his pres. getting his ass beat. I guess not.

"Thanks man, I really appreciate it," Royal says. Shadow pats Royal on the shoulder and turns to head back inside, not even checking on King on his way. I notice two of the hangarounds giving me the evil eye. I think their names are Shawna and Sarah. They chase my guys around like cats in heat, trying to get a piece of them.

"Come on, Princess, let's get you home." Royal takes my hand, leading me to Shadow's truck.

King gets to his feet, yelling out to Royal. "So you're choosing that whore over me? Over your club, your president, your own father? Where did I go wrong with you, boy?"

Royal screeches to a halt, stopping us in our tracks. He lets go of my hand to whip around and face his father.

"What did you just say, old man? Did you not learn anything from the ass-whoopin' that

I just handed you? Did you really just call her a whore? Do we need to go for round two?"

"It is what it is. I'm just callin' it like I see it. And what I see is... A whore." Lucky takes off toward King, but Sinner snatches him up, holding him back from actually making contact.

"This can only end one way. Badly. For all of you boys. Look at you and Lucky. You both are so ready to go to war with me over this slut. How can you not see the way she plays with all of you? You think one day she won't choose one of you and leave the rest of your hearts broken? Everything I've done is to protect you from that. She's nothing but trouble, and you will all get hurt in the end. She walks around like her shit doesn't stink. Like her pussy's made of gold. But I got news for you son. Pussy comes a dime a dozen. She isn't worth what you will lose in the end. Just think about it. You know what I'm saying is true. You're all in a position to take a spot on the council, and you, son, will take over for me one day."

"Just stop, King—" Royal starts, but his father doesn't even hear him.

"Do you think your men will respect you when you're sharing a woman with other club members? Oh, and let's not forget about Dante.

The son of *our* enemy. How exactly does he play into all of this? You aren't using your head, boy. She's always clouded your judgment and I'm just trying to make it easy. For all of you. Your life will be better without her in it."

"Do you think I respect you or that I'd listen to a word you have to say after you just laid your hands on her? If so, you're crazier than you look. You better think twice before you ask me to choose between you and her because I don't think you'll like the answer," Royal viciously proclaims to his father.

Royal turns away from King and leads us to the truck, opening my door for me to get in. That in itself is a statement for King and all the club to witness.

Royal is choosing me. Not that I would ever want him to choose between me and his father or even the club, but he just made it clear to everyone that I come before them.

We ride in silence for a few minutes. The tension filling the cab of the truck is so thick that I'm almost choking on it. "I'm sorry, Royal. I never meant for any of this to happen. I was just angry at him for not telling me you were all okay and keeping me in the dark this whole time. I spent a week outside that clubhouse waiting for one of you to show up. When I finally saw King, he just dismissed me like I was no one and nothing to him. I went months thinking y'all chose to leave me. He could have prevented that. I didn't understand why, but I guess it's pretty clear now. He thinks I'm poison to all of you."

"Stop, Princess. You don't have to explain yourself. I know what he did, and he was wrong. He just didn't like getting called out on it in front of us. He fucked up before he laid his hands on you, and he knew what he was doing. Now he has to face the consequences of his actions." Royal shakes his head, his grip on the wheel tightening, making his knuckles turn white.

I unbuckle my seat belt and scoot next to Royal. He looks at me to see what I'm doing, but I grip his chin and point it back toward the road. Laying down, I rest my head in his lap, so that I'm looking up at him. "You know he's right though."

He looks down at me like I'm crazy and I push his chin back up with my hand. "Eyes on the road, hotshot."

"You need to buckle up."

"I'm not worried about it. I know you'll protect me. I trust you with my life, Royal."

"It's not me I'm concerned with. It's the other idiots on the road."

"Just drive and let me lay here."

"Fine, but what are you talking about? My dad's not right. Nothing he said is true. Don't tell me you actually listened to all the bullshit he was spewing? He's just a crazy old man, Angel. He's set in his ways and he's never understood our relationship. He never will."

"He's not that old. He's not even forty yet. And it wasn't complete bullshit. He had some valid points that we can't just ignore. One of us, or all of us, is bound to get hurt, and the way this is going, it will most likely be all of us. I know you don't wanna hear that, but it's true. Use your head for a second. I mean this one," I say, tapping my finger against his temple. "Not this one." I rub my head against his crotch.

"Be careful with the beast," he jokes, cocking his eyebrow at me. "I don't wanna think about it, but okay, let's say he is right. What does that mean for us? I'm not dumb. I know you have feelings for all of us and we all have feelings for you. So, we all just choose to ignore them."

"What if I don't want to ignore them anymore? I'm sick of ignoring how I feel all the damn time. I've been hiding how I've felt for years, and I'm tired of pretending. I don't care what other people think. I'm just scared that if I allow myself to show all of you how I feel, then I will end up losing all of you. As mad as I was or maybe still am, I can't lose y'all over it. That's the only reason I've suppressed these feelings for so long."

"I don't have the answers you're looking for or even what it means for us, Angel, but what I do know is that I'm not willing to risk losing you forever over it. That has always been a given."

Royal pulls up to my house, parking the truck on the street.

I shift to get up off his lap and he places his hand on my stomach to keep me in place. I toss my head back to his lap a little too hard, hitting his junk and making him jump.

"Fuck, Angel, watch where you put that big-ass melon head of yours. You almost hit the family jewels."

"Yeah, yeah, whatever. Your head is bigger than mine anyway, so I wouldn't be talking, tough guy. And don't think that we're suddenly back to normal just because you defended my honor back there."

Royal pulls me up from his lap. "Come here, Princess."

"I am here," I say, looking at him while questioning his motives.

He grabs my hips and lifts me onto his lap so I'm straddling him. "No, I mean right here." He adjusts the steering wheel so that it isn't shoved into my back.

"Royal—"

"Just give me a minute... please, Princess." He places his forehead against mine, taking a deep breath and exhaling before he continues. "So much has happened, and I just want to be close to you. Even if it's just for a moment. I've missed you more than you'll ever know. These last few months have been hell on earth being away from you. I felt like a piece of my heart was missing. I didn't know if I would ever get it back."

I nod my head against his. "Same, babe. I can't lose you again."

"You won't, and I'm sorry my dad put his hands on you. He was out of line. I'll kill him if he ever thinks about touching you again," he says, running his hand lightly across the area where King hit me. "I'm so sorry, Angel. You deserve better."

"Don't... You didn't do this. King is no better than Gabriel, or maybe he's even worse. Gabriel doesn't pretend to be something he's not. King is a self-righteous bastard trying to play God with our lives."

He runs a hand down his face. Before I can stop myself, I lean forward to place a kiss on his mouth and quickly move back as if it didn't happen. He looks at me, completely shocked. A second passes before he grabs the back of my neck, pulling me forward, and slamming his mouth to mine. The copper taste in his mouth is almost addicting. Knowing it's his battle wound for defending me against his father turns me on. He pulls the hair at the nape of my neck, causing me to grind against him, and coaxing a moan to slip free from me. Royal pulls back all too quickly, trying to catch his breath.

"Come on, Princess, let's get you inside before we start something you aren't ready to finish."

"Who said I'm not ready to finish?" He opens
his door, waiting for me to get off his lap. Frus-
trated, I blow out a loud huff and move to get
out. He closes the truck door behind us and
walks me to the door.

"I have to get back to the clubhouse and deal
with the shit that happened tonight. Maybe another time."

He leans down, giving me a chaste kiss on
the lips before turning back to the truck and
driving off, leaving me horny as hell on my
doorstep. Just wonderful.

Chapter Thirteen

ROYAL

Leaving Angel's house in my rear-view mirror, I fly back to the clubhouse in record time. I'm ready to face the repercussions of what happened tonight. King needs to know where I stand when it comes to Angel, and he needs a reality check about his place in my life. If he has an issue with it, we will deal with it then.

As far as I'm concerned, my father can take his opinions and shove them up his ass.

We all understand that this is a complicated situation. We came to that realization when we were much, much younger.

We all have feelings for Angel. So what? We've learned not to let that come between us, but it will never change the fact that I will die to protect her.

She doesn't deserve King's wrath. And we're not going to just sit back and let him dictate our lives for us anymore. He may be my father and my pres, but this is where I draw the line. He put his fucking hands on my girl and that is not okay. If he can't accept that she will *always* be in my life, then the ass beating I gave him will be just the tip of the fucking iceberg.

I pull up to the clubhouse and park Shadow's truck where he had it before. I make my way inside, finding Sinner, Lucky, and Shadow at the bar shootin' the shit. Walking over to them, I toss Shadow his keys and take a seat beside them.

Lucky spends the next hour trying his best to get all the details about Sinner and Shadow's life out of them. They don't crack or give him anything to work with. But I notice the side-eye they give one another when he mentions a la-dylove.

Hmm, could the stone-cold killers have a special someone waiting at home for them? Naw, that's an insane thought. They spend every waking moment at the club or handling club business. No woman is crazy enough to put up with that.

Cruz slams the door to King's office and strolls straight up to me, grabbing a hold of my shoulder and turning me to face him.

"You need to get outta here until I've calmed him down. He's been holed up in his office since you left. He's on a rampage, Royal. He's been talking about callin' church to have you voted out." He shakes his head at King's nonsense. "I don't agree with any of it. But he's impossible to reason with when he's like this. Just do me a solid and lie low for a few days. In the meantime, I'll try my best to get this straightened out. If you weren't his son, things would be different. Your body would be sitting in the morgue right now," Cruz says, trying to lead me to the door by the arm.

I shake out of his grasp. "If he wasn't my father, I would have unloaded a full clip in his ass. So no, Cruz, I won't go run and hide from my dad like a scared little boy. Fuck that. I appreciate what you're tryin' to do, but he got what was coming to him. The man should count his lucky stars that Jax wasn't here to witness that shit. The damage would be much worse."

I give Cruz a reality check that he's not ready to hear.

"Look, he's just on edge more than ever, right now. With you boys back in town, he's constantly looking around every corner, waiting for Gabriel to make his next move. What he did was wrong, okay. But he's just worried about you boys. Maybe cut him a little slack? He's still your father, Royal. He made a mistake by butting his nose in where it didn't belong." Cruz is interrupted by the slamming of King's office door.

"Is my VP trying to reason with my traitorous son? Did you really just say that I made a mistake? And what mistake would that be, Cruz?" King walks up, shoving Cruz hard in the chest. Sinner and Shadow have stayed back until this point, but they immediately hop off their barstools and head our way. Lucky swivels around on his own stool to get a good look. With his beer in one hand, he raises it high for a second, like he's just here for the show.

Asshole.

Cruz steps up to face King. "It's my job to keep the peace, so that's what I'm doing. If you got a problem with that, then maybe you should find yourself a new VP. One who will put up with your temper tantrums. Your arrogance is at an all-time high, King. I didn't sign up to play therapist to you and your boy."

"Is that an official resignation? Because it sounds to me as if it is." King looks around, waiting for someone to back him up. "Isn't that what it sounds like to you, boys?"

King turns on me, grabbing me by my cut and tries to rip it off of me. I shove him back. "What the fuck is your problem? Get off me." He reeks of alcohol and is stumbling around like a fool.

"You don't deserve to wear this cut. You're pathetic. Chasin' after some pussy who doesn't even want your sorry-ass. She wants all your little friends instead. And you're going to dis-respect me and my club over that whore? I am your flesh and blood. I can't even stand to look at you right now. I didn't raise you this way, boy."

"I don't give a damn who you are! If you ever put your hands on another woman in front of me again, being disrespected is the last thing you'll need to worry about. You raised me to do right by people. But apparently your morals got lost somewhere down the line." I'm disgusted by him at this point. "If you wanna cry about it like a little bitch, then do that, but just know you won't toss me out of this club unless we take it to church. If the vote falls in your favor, then I'll happily take my ass somewhere that I'm wanted."

Lucky jumps off the barstool where he had happily planted his ass during this shit show. He strides over to us. "How about both of you just calm the fuck down. No disrespect, King, but you're making an ass out of yourself for the whole club to see. And Royal, brother, let's take a walk. I think we've all had enough drama for one night."

"How is Lucky the reasonable one in all this?" Shadow laughs, turning away from us. He takes up his seat back at the bar, ordering a round of shots from Shawna who's now pouring drinks.

"Fine. Let's go, Luck," I say, walking out the door, not waiting for him to follow.

He's a few steps behind me as we head outside. I turn around, raising my eyebrows in question. "Since when did you become the peacemaker? And why aren't you just as pissed off as I am? He put his fucking hands on Angel, Luck. I mean, come the fuck on." I try to rile him up.

"Yeah, I know. I was the one holding Angel in my arms while you beat the fuck out of your dad. I saw red the same as you. Do you actually think I'm not as pissed off as you are about it all? Do you think I didn't want to do the same thing you did, or even worse? But let's be real. At the end of the day, he's still your father and our president. I've looked up to that man my whole life, then in a blink of an eye, I lost every bit

189

of respect I ever had for him. I'm not about to make a move against him with the whole club watching. I'm crazy, but not that crazy. You may be able to get away with that shit because you're his son, but to most of the guys in there, I'm just another prospect."

"I'm sorry, Luck. I didn't mean to question your loyalty like that. I know you love Angel and would protect her with your life. It's just after everything we put her through these last few months it's getting to me, you know? I let my dad keep us away then witnessed him putting his hands on her. It all just made me feel like this is my fault or something. I just know that I'll do whatever it takes to protect her from all this bullshit. We owe her that much."

Lucky pulls me in for a quick hug. "We will protect her, Royal. We just need a plan to keep your dad away from her and out of our business. And fuck, don't get me started on keeping Gabriel's slimy ass away from her."

"What are you talking about? What did I miss? Has Gabriel been going after Angel? Why the fuck am I just now hearing about this? Not that she's been speaking to any of us unless we force her to, but if he's doing something to her, then I need to know."

"One problem at a time, bro. One at a damn time. Come on, let's go check the property." He slaps me on the shoulder and we walk toward the back of the Reapers' property line.

The Reapers' property is twenty acres surrounded by an eight-foot iron fence with barbed wire on top for protection.

The actual clubhouse sits near the main road for easy access. The auto body repair shop, plus the coffee shop, also sit near the main road, but that's just to help keep up appearances. At the back of the property are several abandoned buildings where we stockpile anything we can get our hands on. Drugs, guns, you name it, we probably have it stored in one of those buildings.

The prospects are tasked with inventory and surveillance of the buildings. No one's ever known about it outside the Reapers. Not even the cops, even though they come sniffing around here from time to time.

Lucky and I walk around the property for hours. Talking about everything that we've been through lately and how we can make it up to Angel.

We reach the clubhouse and head inside for another drink. It's the middle of the night, so most of the members and hangarounds have cleared out.

Sinner and Shadow are sitting on the couch having a heated conversation about something. They're keeping their voices to a whisper, but you can tell by their body language that whatever they are discussing is pretty serious.

I head around the bar and grab a couple of beers for Luck and myself, and we head to the sitting area to join Sinner and Shadow. Luck plops down between the two of them, crowding their space and interrupting their conversation.

"What are you two grumps so serious about?" Luck says, trying to lighten the mood.

The guys shake their heads at him because he obviously has an issue with personal boundaries. These guys hate people being in their space. I chuckle as I take a seat in the chair across from them.

Just as I get comfortable, the ground begins to shake, the windows start to rattle and then comes a boom.

Red and orange light casts shadows everywhere as we rush outside to see what's going on.

Chapter Fourteen

ANGEL

"Are you ready for round two, sweetheart?" Gabriel asks, making me jump at the sound of his voice and scaring me half to death. This does not help the fact that I'm already on edge from today's escapades. Now he's here in my house, uninvited, once again.

"What the fuck, Gabriel? What are you doing here? You can't keep doing this shit." I yell at him as I walk over to flip on the lights. When the lights flash on, I find him sprawled out on my couch, making himself comfortable in my home. It's safe to say this is becoming a bit of a habit for him.

"The last time I checked, I do what the fuck I want, when I want. I don't go around asking for permission. I just thought after today you might be interested in round two." He jumps off the couch, striding toward me, taking my chin in his hand, and turning my head to the side so he can get a better look at the damage.

"Better question, sweetheart. Who the fuck hit you?" He pushes a strand of my hair behind my ear, then runs the back of his hand down my cheek. A hiss escapes me as he moves over the spot where I was struck, and he backs away a few inches to inspect the area. His facial features morph from a teasing expression into a scowl as he lets out a low growl. "Who am I killing tonight?"

"Umm, thanks but no thanks. There will be no killing of anyone on my behalf. It was handled. Besides, there's enough bloodshed in this town. I don't want or need any of that on my hands." I slap his hand away from my face and walk away, heading to the kitchen. He follows closely behind me as I grab a glass from the cupboard to pour myself a drink.

"Why are you here? Between you shooting up the diner and getting backhanded by... I think I'm at my limit for douchebag run-ins today. Maybe try again tomorrow? Or shit, better yet, don't."

"I may be a lot of things, but a woman abuser ain't one of them. That's something I'm not okay with, Angel," he says, taking a step closer to me, causing me to take a step back.

"Murderer, torturer, drug dealer, stalker, and a horrible-ass parent...check. Not a woman abuser, that's where you draw the line. Duly noted." I sigh deeply, shaking my head at him. "Who hurt you, Angel? Whoever did this deserves to be six feet under, and you're just in luck because that's my specialty," he says sternly.

I laugh mockingly. "You. You hurt me, over and over again. You forbid Dante from being in my life, which tore my heart in two. Then I find out you're the reason the guys had to go into hiding, which completely fucked with my head. Therefore, YOU are the person behind the majority of the hurt and pain in my life. Should I continue, or does that answer your question? Are you going to kill yourself now or are you all talk?" I snarl at him.

I need a shower, my comfortable bed, and twelve hours of sleep. I don't need this jerk demanding answers that I know I shouldn't give him.

He slams his hand against the cabinets, making me jump. "I get it. I'm the bad guy. The reason your precious little boy toys left you. Tell them to grow a pair and man the fuck up instead of hiding like little cowards from the big bad wolf. Don't worry though, I'll find the three little piggies in due time. Now tell me, who the fuck hit you?" He takes another step forward, crowding my space again, trapping me between the wall and his muscular chest.

"What does it matter, Gabriel? I'm not your concern. Why do you care anyway? A woman with bruises on her face or blood spilled in the streets. Sounds like a regular ol' Tuesday night in Imperial Beach to me."

"Don't be a brat, Angel. You want me to leave? Fine, give me a name and I'll be on my way," he demands, waving his hand at the door.

"I'm not telling you anything, Gabriel, so you might as well just leave now."

He huffs and shakes his head.

Before I even have a chance to figure out what's going on, he swoops down and picks me up. Cradling me in his arms, he makes his way toward my bedroom.

"What the fuck? Put me down, asshole," I scream, slapping at his arms and chest to get away from him.

"Chill the fuck out before you make me drop you on your ass."

He enters my room, heading into the bathroom, and drops me to my feet. Then goes to turn on the water, confusing the hell out of me. He checks the water temperature, then grabs my foaming bath Epsom salt and pours it into the tub. He walks over to me, grabs the hem of my shirt, and pulls it off as I stand here in shock.

"Do I need to take the rest off or are you capable of doing that without a fight?" he asks.

"You confuse the hell out of me, you know that, right?" I strip down, not caring that he's getting an eyeful of my naked body.

I move to the tub and dip my foot into the water. It feels like heaven. The water is perfect. I step in, letting my body get used to the warmth.

"Join the club, sweetheart. I confuse myself most of the time," he says, moving to sit against the wall next to the tub. "Just relax and enjoy your bath. Wash that blood off you while you're at it." Pulling his knees up and resting his arms over them, he lays his head on his arms before he continues to speak. "Look, I don't know why I care, either. But when you turned on that light and I saw you with a bruise on your face and blood on your clothes, anger just took over. I want to protect you or something. I don't know how to explain it. I showed up with the hopes of seducing you again after our little rendezvous in the alley today. I wasn't expecting to find you in this state. It kind of threw a wrench in my plans, ya know?"

I'm not sure how to respond to that. He has my mind spinning more than it already was. Where he's concerned, anyway. "It wasn't my blood."

"Well, I guess that's a good thing. At least you made the fucker bleed." He bobs his head like he's proud of that.

"I didn't. I prefer not to use violence to handle my issues, but it all happened so fast.," I trail off, not wanting to give him too much information.

"Says the girl with a thousand soldiers, ready and willing to go into battle for her. Which one of your boyfriends stepped up to the plate? And before you try to lie, yes, I already know that they are back in town."

Well shit, he knows they're back, which can only mean one thing. War is coming.

"Please don't hurt the guys, Gabe. I'm begging you. I know what happened, and I'm truly sorry about your brother, but please don't take them from me. I'm not sure I would survive that. I'll do anything. Just don't take them from me again." I pour out the words in my heart, pleading with him as tears burn the back of my eyes.

He rubs his chin, thinking it over. "That's a big ask, Angel. Royal killed my brother, and I can't just let him walk away unscathed. It would make me look weak in front of the club. I can't risk that. King would take it as a sign of weakness and come after me and the Sons. And let's say, he got wind of me letting Royal off because of you. That gives him one more reason to eliminate you from all of our lives. Royal is following in his father's footsteps. He may not walk the path in a straight line, but he's close enough that it won't be long before Royal becomes the same kind of man that King is. I'm sorry, Angel. You don't deserve to be in the middle of this war. But that's exactly where you are."

We sit quietly for a few minutes. Neither of us know what to say. Gabriel breaks the silence first. "You know, Angel, there are different types of monsters in this world. The kind like me who aren't afraid to show you exactly who we are, not fearing what people have to say about it, and right or wrong, we own up to it. Then you have others who wear a mask. They make people believe they are good, when in reality, they are the worst kind of monsters. They pull you in, make you believe you can trust them, that they care for you, and when they show what kind of monster they really are, it hits you differently. You're blindsided by their cruel ways, and it feels like you've been hit by a semi going a hundred miles an hour. It can be devastating and set you back. For people like me and you, it makes us doubt everything and everyone. Even the ones closest to us."

He raises his head, opening his eyes and looking straight at me. "We learn from those betrayals more than anything else we experience in life. We grow thicker and tougher skin, vowing to not be like them. For some, it's easier to wear that mask because they are deceivers at heart, manipulating others while anticipating their downfall all along. You don't have to tell me who hit you if you don't trust me, but make sure you learn from this. You are a beautiful girl with a spirit that calls to many. There will be people who will try to destroy you for those reasons alone."

I take a deep breath, processing his words. He's right. King is a different kind of monster. Gabriel wears his crazy on his sleeve. There's no doubt about it. But King? No, he wants you to believe he's your friend. Your savior. Your protector. He didn't think twice when he hit me, or about the awful things he said. He kept the guys away, and who knows what else he's done that we aren't aware of.

We've always thought of Gabriel as the devil, but maybe King is the true devil in disguise.

I sink my head down into the water to collect my thoughts. When I come back up, I turn to look at Gabriel, who has a slight smirk on his face. I smile back at him and rest my head against the tub. Closing my eyes I whisper, "It was King." I glance over at Gabriel to see his reaction as he starts to chuckle and begins bobbing his head as if he knew. He isn't as shocked by this information as I expected.

"So the monster in my story has now become yours. I wasn't expecting you to say that or to actually tell me, but I'm also not surprised. King has this whole town fooled. Not that I need another reason to kill him, but it's a reminder of why he needs to be put down like the dog he is."

"Why do you care what he does to me? You've spent the last three months stalking me and invading my privacy in every imaginable way. Now I'm supposed to believe you care who smacks me around? I don't buy it."

"Last time I checked, invading your privacy wasn't the same as smacking you around. I don't know what it is, but something about you draws me in. Even when I know it shouldn't. Now, that same thing has me wanting to protect you. At least from King."

"I shouldn't be shocked by what he did, but honestly, I am. I thought King was family. Growing up, I looked at him like a father, but after these past few months, I should've known better. I swear no one in this god-forsaken town can be trusted. Are you going to tell me what happened between you and King? Why do you hate him so much, anyway?"

"King destroyed my family. We grew up together. Did you know that? He was my best friend when we were younger. What he did cut me deep. Maybe one day I'll tell you the whole story, but not tonight. You've been through enough today, and I'm partly to blame for that." He stands up and makes his way to the door. "Finish your bath and get some rest."

"Thanks for this. I'm still not sure why you care but thank you. It was nice having someone take care of me, even if it was for only a moment."

He heads out of the bathroom, and I hear the door close behind him. I lean back and let myself relax for the first time this evening. A few minutes later, a knock comes from the front door. I get out of the bath, wrap my towel around me, and head toward the sound.

"Did you all of a sudden find your manners?" I say as I open the door, thinking it's Gabriel.

Jax shoves the door open. He and Dante barge into my house with me standing there in nothing but a towel.

"You wanna explain what the fuck my dad is doing leaving your house at this time of night? And with you looking like that?" Dante yells at me.

"Umm, not really," I blurt out, moving to open the door so they can let themselves out. Dante slams it shut again.

"Fuck that. You don't get to do that, Angel. Why was my dad here? Did he do that to your face?"

Jax responds before I get the opportunity. "No, that was courtesy of King. I came straight over after Royal called to let me know what went down. He told me to come check on you because he didn't want you to be alone, but you weren't alone, were you?"

"What are you two doing here? I've had about all the drama I can take for one night. So, if you don't mind, I'd like to get in bed and try to regain some of the sanity I lost today."

Jax steps toward me. "Don't answer a question with a question, Trouble. I hate when you do that. It's also one of your tells when you know you're doing something you shouldn't be," he explains.

"Lucky called to let me know what happened at the diner with Gabriel. I wanted to come check on you, so I parked around the corner and walked up through the side. Apparently, Jax was also coming to check on you when he saw Gabriel walk out the front door like he owned the damn place. What was he doing here, and why are you soaking wet and answering the door in a towel when he just left?" Dante sounds hurt and confused. "Did you sleep with him, Angel?"

"I didn't sleep with him, Dante. When Royal dropped me off tonight, he was already in the house. Sneaking in is apparently his new hobby." I don't like hiding things from them, but I'm worried what my honestly will cost me this time.

"So, this isn't the first time he's snuck in?" Jax asks, raising his eyebrows at me.

"No, it's not the first time and I doubt it will be the last. Can we move this party into the bedroom so I can dry off and get dressed, please?" I ask, walking away from them.

They enter the room as I'm shuffling through my drawers trying to find something to throw on. Jax pulls me away from the dresser and into his arms, holding me tight.

"I'm sorry I wasn't there tonight, Trouble. None of that shit would have gone down if I would have been. King's a dead man. Fuck the club and fuck anyone that says otherwise. He won't get away with hurting you. He's caused enough damage," Jax breathes into the side of my head as he squeezes me, trying to give me some sort of comfort.

"We will figure out how to deal with King together, Jax. I don't want you taking on my battles when you all have enough on your plate right now."

Jax takes my chin and slowly, but hesitantly, guides my lips to his. His kiss is soft at first, but when I open up, it becomes more demanding. His grip tightens as his other hand travels down my body to my ass, giving it a squeeze while pulling me closer.

"Ugh, hello? I'm still standing here. You know what? Fuck it. I'm out. I can't watch this," Dante says, turning to walk out of the bedroom.

I quickly break my kiss with Jax to grab Dante's bicep, pulling him toward me. I wrap my arms around him, telling him that I'm sorry. I'm not sure how to handle this, but I know that I don't want Dante to leave.

"Trouble, just let him go if he wants to leave," Jax says, taking my arm off Dante and pulling me back to him.

"I don't want either of you to leave. Today's been insane, I'm exhausted and I'd rather not be alone. My mom is at work for the night. So will you both just stay with me?"

"I'm not going anywhere," Jax says, eyeing me mischievously.

"Well, if you're not leaving, then neither am I," Dante challenges.

"So, what now? Talk or sleep? Please, say sleep," I suggest, even though my body is dying to be in the middle of them.

"If sleep is what you want, then sleep is what you get. Come on, Trouble." Jax grabs my nightgown off the back of my bathroom door and holds it out, waiting for me to slip it on. Once it's on, I drop my towel from underneath and climb into bed. The guys strip down to their boxers, climbing in and laying on either side of me. This should make for an interesting night. Saying goodnight, I close my eyes trying not to stress over the conversation I need to have with the guys about Gabe, and start to drift off to Neverland.

Chapter Fifteen

ANGEL

Warm hands rub up and down my thighs, making me arch my back and causing my ass to move back, only to collide with a rock-solid cock. I let out a needy moan as fingers slip underneath my nightgown, massaging a path up my body. A gentle hand pulls my hair to the side, as hot breath fans over my ear. "Keep it down, Trouble, unless you want to wake up Dante," he whispers.

I slowly grind my ass against his hard length. Jax's touch feels so familiar and good on my body. He snakes his hand around me, making his way up to my breasts and caressing them. He slides his thumb over my nipple and gives it a tug, causing us both to moan. Dante starts to stir in his sleep, making us both freeze until he settles.

Jax's hand skates across my stomach and down to my naked pussy. He teases my lips for a second before slipping a finger inside me, gliding it in and out.

His mouth finds my neck, kissing it, and swirling his tongue around before he starts to suck. He leaves a trail of little hickeys down my neck to my shoulder, marking me as his. As much as I try, I can't help the sounds coming from me. I bury my face in the pillow and spread my legs further, so he can continue his pursuit. Jax ignites a burning desire inside and breathes life into my soul. My body is begging for a release and his hands are doing everything right. He circles my clit with his thumb, and as he inserts a second finger, I rock my hips, instinctively riding his hand to capture my pleasure quickly.

Dante turns over in his sleep, facing me with his eyes still closed. That doesn't stop my movements. I need this, and I need it now. I feel the pressure inside me building up as Jax curls his fingers, hitting that sweet spot in my core. He sends me over the edge and makes my body shake uncontrollably.

"Fuck." I muffle my scream into the pillow as the orgasm takes over. Jax is relentless. He doesn't stop until my body starts to relax.

He glides his fingers out of me and licks them clean.

"Shit, I need more, so much more," he says, pulling the blanket over his head and sliding slowly down the bed.

"What are you doing?" I whisper as he moves under the covers, grabbing my leg and rolling me onto my back. Then he dives in.

He licks from my ass to clit before plunging his tongue deep into my opening. My body is still reeling from the last orgasm as he devours me.

I grab ahold of Jax's head, trying to wrap my fingers in his short, hair to push him deeper. My legs unknowingly wrap around him. It's like my body has a mind of its own. Jax is circling my lips, teasing my hole with every move. He licks up to my clit, flicking his tongue rapidly across it, then back to my opening, shoving his tongue deep inside me. "Fuck. Jax. I'm gonna come."

He grabs ahold of my ass, tilting it to give him a better angle. I'm so lost in my pleasure that I don't even notice that Dante woke up at some point. It isn't until I feel his hand glide across my stomach up to my breast that I turn to look at him.

He pulls me into a deep passionate kiss, which only heightens all of my senses.

Jax stops what he's doing to throw the blanket off of us. "About fucking time. You sleep like the dead, dude." I hear him chuckle before he dips his head and continues ravishing my lady bits. I've never felt this good before. It's like I'm having an out-of-body experience. At least I wish I were, so I could get a good look at the two of them carrying me across the finish line one more fucking time.

My orgasm takes me by surprise as it explodes from my body. This time, there's no need to hold back. So I don't. I grip Jax's hair tight and ride his face to kingdom come.

Dante sucks on my breasts, giving them equal attention as Jax licks the last of my cum and sits up, trying to get a good look at us.

"Trouble, who knew you were a squirter?" Jax chuckles, kissing the inside of my thigh.

I playfully smack his arm, "Am not. Take that back, right now."

"Oh, you are, baby girl. Maybe you just haven't had the right person go down on you, but the evidence is all over my face. It's not a bad thing, babe."

He looks from me to Dante. "How about we see if I can make it happen again, this time on my dick." He pulls his dick out and begins stroking it. "What do you say, D? Wanna make Trouble ours?"

"She's always been ours. I guess we might as well make it official. What do you say, Heaven? You down? Can you handle both of us?"

I look between them, their cocks about equal in size, and I'm not sure how this will work, but I nod anyway. "I've never done this before, but I think I want to try."

"We can go as fast or as slow as you need us to. If you decide you want us to stop, then just say the word and we will," Jax assures me, which helps settle my nerves.

"Uh, have you guys done this before? Like together with another girl?"

I'm not sure I want the answer, but they seem so comfortable at the thought of sharing. It makes me think this isn't their first time.

"No," they answer simultaneously. I release the breath I didn't realize I've been holding.

"Thank God. I was starting to get second thoughts if this was something you normally do."

They both chuckle as they settle into place. Jax spreads my thighs as I wrap my legs around his waist, and he laughs as I push him closer to my entrance. "Someone's impatient."

Dante gets undressed and slowly starts stroking himself as he looks between me and Jax. "You sure you don't want me to go first? This wouldn't be our first time."

Oh Lord, here comes the pissing contest.

Jax and I burst into laughter at the same time. "Umm, what makes you think this is our first time?" he asks, as he positions his cock at my opening and slides in with ease from my wetness. His thick cock stretches me to the max. "Fuck, baby, you feel so good," Jax groans.

He moves his hips and I look over at Dante to see when he's going to join the party. He has a confused look on his face. Jax stops moving to address Dante. "I was her first, bro. Ya know, before you decided to mix shit up. No need to look so concerned. Did you really never stop to think about why I flipped out the way I did when I saw you two together?"

"Wow. No, I didn't. I just thought you were being your usual overbearing asshole self. I guess it makes sense now," Dante responds.

"Uhh, hello, we're in the middle of something here. Can we talk about that later? I'd really like to focus on the task at hand. You know, giving me another orgasm. Soon, please."

Someone's lost the plot and it ain't me.

"Your wish is my command, baby," Jax claims, flipping me over onto all fours and slamming his thick length inside of me, making me yell out from the sudden movement.

Asshole.

I grab a hold of Dante, stroking him firmly. I pull him by the thighs closer to me so that I can take him in my mouth. He scoots toward me and takes a handful of my hair, pulling tight. "Look at me, Heaven. I'm going to fuck that pretty little mouth and you are going to take it like a good girl, aren't you?" Excitement fills my body as I slip my tongue out, licking him from base to tip and back down. I wrap my lips around him and hum on his dick in agreement.

Jax slaps my ass hard, forcing me to take Dante further, almost making me choke on his cock. He begins rubbing the spot where his hand landed, soothing away the sting.

"Open wide. I'm going to fuck your mouth the same way Jax fucks that tight pussy of yours." I do as he commands, relaxing my jaw to give him complete control.

Dante pushes his cock deeper inside of me. He hits the back of my throat several times before I start to gag and get sloppy with it. His thumb slides across my cheek, wiping away the tears streaming down it. "You're fucking perfect, baby," Dante claims.

I look up, meeting his piercing blue eyes. He tilts his head to the side and slows his strokes. "I've been wondering something all night, Heaven." I try pulling back to respond, but he grips my hair tight and pushes back into my mouth. "I didn't say stop what you're doing, did I?" He breaks eye contact to look at Jax. "Jaxy has probably been wondering the same thing." He looks back down at me. "Did my father touch you?"

Oh FUCK!

Jax comes to a halt, and my eyes widen in shock.

I can't believe he's asking that RIGHT. NOW. Fuck, what do I do? Our relationship may never recover if they catch me in a lie, but if I tell them the truth, I could still lose them all in an instant.

Jax slams his cock deep inside of me. "We need an answer, Trouble," he says with a forceful stroke that has me gasping for air.

Dante uses my silence against me, shoving his cock all the way down my throat. I lift my hand to his hip and shove him back a little. His dick falls out of my mouth with a pop. "Yes, assholes, he did."

Dante yanks my head back, forcing me to look up at him. He takes his dick in the other hand and starts tapping my lips with it. "Open. The. Fuck. Up. Angel," he demands. Slowly I open my mouth to him, knowing this will be brutal. I've never seen this side of Dante, forceful and demanding. As weird as it may sound, I kind of like it. He lets me lick his shaft and tip before I begin to suck him off. He must be lost in thought because he lets me have control for a minute. Jax, on the other hand, does not.

Jax quickly pulls out of me. He takes the side of his hand, running it over my clit and through the juices on my lips. "Did he touch you here?"

When I don't immediately respond, Jax slaps my pussy, sending electric shock waves through my entire body. I moan loudly around Dante's cock.

Jax leans over my back, putting his mouth right up to my ear, "Answer me, Angel."

I slightly nod my head as Jax runs his cock through my wetness. "You fucked him?" He pauses, waiting for my response. I mumble what I hope sounds like no.

Dante snaps out of his trance and grabs me by the hair, pulling out of my mouth. "But he touched you? Did you like it? Is that why he's sneaking over here?"

"Fuck. No. Yes. I don't know. It's all super confusing," I respond.

"Did he touch you with his fingers?" Dante asks, while Jax inserts what feels like three or more fingers inside of me.

I moan loudly, "Yes."

"Did he touch you with his mouth?" Dante asks, as Jax pulls his hand away and replaces it with his tongue on my clit.

"Fuck. Yes. Yes, he did."

"But he didn't fuck you? Are you lying to me, Angel? Did you let Gabriel stick his dirty dick inside that sweet pussy of yours?"

Jax abruptly stops his assault on my clit to push himself up. I try to catch my breath to respond, "Noooooo. Fuck, y'all are assholes. You know that, right?" Jax buries his dick so deep inside me I think I can feel it in my throat.

Dante grabs me by the hair, twisting it around his hand for leverage. Opening up, I let him have his way with me. He deserves that much after the bomb I just dropped.

Jax takes the opportunity to smack my ass cheek as he slams into me. "Your pussy's so magical, even the devil wants a taste. Too bad for him because it's all mine." They are both pushing me to my limit, and it feels amazing.

"Ours," Dante corrects him. "I'm about to nut Angel, and you're going to swallow every last drop. Own my dick the same way I own that delicious pussy of yours."

That's the only warning I get before he spills his seed on my tongue and down my throat. I pull back slightly.

Keeping the tip of him on my lips, I open wide, showing him his cum on my tongue before I swallow it. Using his thumb, he wipes the last bit of it off my lip and pushes it into my mouth for me to suck clean.

Jax pulls out of me suddenly and flips me onto my back. "Oh, no. I'm not done with you yet." He throws my legs over his shoulders and guides himself back into me. My pussy clenches around him and he moans loudly. I feel my orgasm on the horizon. "Faster, Jax. Harder," I demand with heavy breaths, needing to find my release. Dante slips his hand between us and begins circling my clit, pushing me higher and higher toward my climax. Jax spreads my legs, pounding my pussy with no regard.

My body explodes with pleasure from these gods among men. My vision blurs and then I'm left with stars in the darkness. Jax claims my soul with a few last strokes before he comes hard, filling my core with his seed.

Coming down from my intense high, I notice we're both shaking. I turn to see Dante stroking his hard cock just before his cum shoots across my chest.

The guys collapse beside me, each of them taking a side. "Fuck, that was by far the hottest thing I've ever been a part of," Jax says.

Come morning, I'll have hell to pay. But right now? I'm in a state of pure bliss.

Just as we are about to close our eyes, ready to pass out, Dante's and Jax's phones start buzzing. "It's probably just Luck making sure you're okay. I'll call him back in the morning." Jax breathes.

Both men snuggle up against me, and their phones start to buzz repeatedly, only this time mine starts ringing along with theirs.

Jax gets off the bed to fetch our phones. He tosses Dante his first, and I catch a glimpse of Gabriel's name as he holds it up for a brief second before placing it under his pillow. Jax takes his phone from his jeans and turns it around to let me see Lucky's name flashing across the screen before he presses the green button to accept the call.

"Hey man, what's up?" he answers. I can't make out what Lucky is saying on the other end of the line, but he sounds distraught. "Fuck! Yeah, I'm at Angel's now. She's okay." He tries to lower his voice as I hear the clicking of his volume button.

"We can talk about that later. I'm on my way. I'll be there as soon as I can." Jax says, ending the call as he starts to get dressed.

"What's up?" Dante asks.

"Nothing. Club business," he snaps back at Dante.

"Gotcha. So none of our business is what you really mean," Dante huffs, falling back on his pillow.

"No worries. I'll keep Heaven's mind occupied while you go handle that." He wraps his arm around me, pulling me into his side.

"I'm sure you will, fucker." Sounding agitated that he's being pulled away, he leans forward to give me a kiss goodbye before quickly turning to walk away.

Dante's phone vibrates from under the pillow again. He must have put it on silent when he saw Gabriel's name. "Just ignore it. He'll stop calling eventually," he says. The phone stops for a total of one second before it starts up again.

"Just answer it," I tell him.

He huffs loudly, snatching his phone. "It's the middle of the night. What could you possibly want right now, Gabriel? What? When? Fuck! Zeke, slow down. I'm on my way." Dante hangs up and starts to get dressed, turning to look at me with sadness and confusion written across his face. "My dad's been shot. I've got to go."

Chapter Sixteen

GABRIEL

KABOOM!

I stand back, watching the embers fall from the sky. The taste of vengeance is so sweet. I've known about the Reapers' secret hiding spot for a while now. I've spent a lot of time and resources putting together what I need to make this happen. From the intel that I've gathered, they have almost all of their gun supply in these abandoned buildings, along with a huge amount of drugs supplied by the Castro Cartel.

All of it just went up in flames, thanks to yours truly.

That one was for Viper. The next one's for me. Getting the revenge I've sought after for all these years will be a nice victory to hold over the Reapers, or what's left of them.

Let's see King try to wiggle his way out of this one.

Hidden in the forest surrounding the Reapers' property is a path that the boys and I take back to our bikes.

"Are you sure that we didn't leave anything behind?" Zeke questions Cain and me as we enter the woods.

"We got it all," Cain responds. Cain is the best Sergeant-at-Arms the Sons have ever seen. He enforces the bylaws and makes sure I'm protected at all times. I tend to make his job harder when I sneak off for late night house calls, but he never complains or questions me about what I'm doing. Well, he didn't until tonight, anyway.

The two of them signed up for this suicide mission without even blinking.

The rest of the guys are back at the club waiting for the word from us so they can begin their part of this plan. We lost too many men this year, and we can't afford another big hit like last time. Losing my brother changed me, and not for the better.

I wish I could stick around to see King's reaction, but I have other places that I need to be. King and the rest of the Reapers will be on damage control with the cartel for at least the next few days. Which should buy me a little more time to execute my plan.

"Let's go, boys. You know what to do from here. We need to rendezvous back at the meeting point in no less than four hours. That should give everyone enough time to hit their targets and get the hell out of town before the Reapers have time to realize what's going on."

"Are you sure about this, Boss? The next move might be the final nail in that coffin of yours and Dante's relationship," Cain asks, looking worried. He steps toward me, placing his hand on my shoulder, giving it a squeeze for comfort. "We can think of another way if you decide not to go through with it. This doesn't have to be the only option. We can think of something else while the Reapers are scrambling to recover."

I eye his hand, giving it a look of disgust. Cain quickly removes it.

As we finally approach our bikes, I look between Zeke and Cain, thinking of all the ways this could go wrong for any one of us. We've come this far, so there's no turning back now. The time to discuss other options has long passed. The moment we lit the fuse on those bombs we placed, our decision was solidified.

Cain comes up beside me, breaking my train of thought. "It's your call. Just tell us what to do here."

"We stick to the plan. I won't undo everything just because Dante will be upset in the end. I'm pretty sure he's hated me for many years now. What's a few more?" I reply.

"Alright then. Good luck, Boss. Y'all watch your six," Zeke says as he jumps on his bike and takes off.

Cain and I race toward our first target. A few minutes later, we pull onto the side street beside the Reapers' safe house.

The windows are all blacked out or boarded up so that we can't see inside them. I pray the information we received from my mole isn't wrong. Otherwise, this could get nasty real quick.

King uses this house to run drugs for the cartel. Most of the club members are unaware of its existence or King's deal with the cartel. Only a few low-level guys that need extra cash know about this. King went to them, knowing they were in a financial bind and offered them a way to help support their families. You can't really say no to that. Even if it means finding low lives to help you push drugs. Also, it leaves you without the protection of the club at your back.

If you ask me, it's pretty dumb, and a careless move at that. One that I'm completely comfortable using to my advantage.

"You take the back and I'll head around the front. Remember, once it's set you'll have sixty seconds to clear the area before it detonates. Don't wait for the smoke to clear and don't pull the trigger unless it's necessary," I explain to Cain.

"Got it," Cain says as he moves toward the back of the house.

I quickly move to the front, climbing the stairs and setting the bomb in place. Once it's set, I haul ass off the porch, back around the side. I draw my gun as I wait patiently. The explosions go off like clockwork, almost simultaneously.

The front door comes off its hinges, leaving the entryway exposed. Heading inside, I check to my left, then right, as I move into the living room. Cain comes from the back of the house dragging a body behind him. "He's unconscious. Not dead," he reassures me. These men don't deserve to die just because they trusted the wrong guy. I've been there and I'm still dealing with the fallout.

"Watch him. I'll check out the rest of the house," Cain says, taking his position far too seriously.

I reach for his arm to stop his movement. I place a finger over my lips to signal him to be quiet as I move the two of us to the side and out of view from the hallway. I hear shuffling coming from one of the bedrooms. The door squeaks as it opens. Whoever this is, they're definitely not trained in the art of stealth. Heavy footsteps pound across the wooden floors.

The barrel of a shotgun comes into view as I quietly exhale, waiting for the right moment to attack.

The guy takes one more step forward before I make my move. I grab the barrel with my left hand, aiming it toward the ceiling. His jaw meets the full force of my right hook only a second later.

A lesser man would have easily gone down without a fight, but not him.

I consider myself a big guy, but he's a few inches taller than I am and has at least twenty pounds on me. He didn't even stumble when I hit him.

We scrabble for possession of the shotgun just as Cain tries to wrap his arms up from behind him. He tosses Cain to the side like a ragdoll and head butts me as hard as he can, catching me in the nose. I hear the crunch before the pain radiates through my face.

Yeah, I'm pretty sure that's going to leave a mark.

The tough motherfucker throws a couple of punches to my ribs then back at my face. I'm giving as much as I get, but it's not making a dent in this guy's stamina. He doesn't quit. He just keeps coming for me.

Cain gets up off the ground and runs over to us. He throws himself on the guy's back and pounds his head in while I attack his body. The man tries to throw Cain off but falls to his knees instead. I'm quick to take advantage of his misstep. I throw my knee into his face over and over again until the fight leaves him and he falls to the ground.

Cain rolls off of him breathing heavily. "Fuck, I was not prepared for that guy."

"Me neither, but we've wasted enough time with him. Let's drag their asses out back and tie them up before we have any other surprises," I respond, grabbing the first guy's legs and dragging him to the back door.

Cain follows with the big one. Once we make it to the backyard, Cain grabs the supplies and starts to tie them up farther from the house.

As soon as I see that he has this handled, I run back inside to do a sweep of the house, checking for money or guns. The drugs can burn with the rest of the house as far as I'm concerned. I find the duffle bag loaded with cash, a couple of pistols, and the shotgun that we struggled over. I toss them out the back door and move into the front room to set the charge.

The house goes up in flames seconds later, destroying all the drugs that King was hiding there. If he wants to make a big deal out of it, then he'll have to explain what he's been up to this whole time to his men.

Cain and I leave the guys tied up in the backyard. Someone will eventually find them. We hightail it out of there to meet Zeke for the exchange. He's right on the border of town but close enough to our next destination.

We pull into the parking lot of the gas station to fill up our bikes. We have a long drive ahead of us, so we need to be prepared.

"How'd it go?" Zeke asks, looking at my blood-stained clothes.

"We ran into a small problem, but thanks to Cain's quick thinking we managed to get out quickly. After that, it went off with a bang," I reply, throwing him a mischievous wink.

He nods his head, clapping me on the shoulder. "I'm glad you're both okay."

Cain hands Zeke the duffle bag as he carefully places a small bag in the palm of my hand.

"Small doses, you hear me? This stuff is strong enough to keep an elephant down for several hours," he explains. I pull out the small liquid vile to look it over before placing it back in the bag and into my jacket pocket for safe keeping.

"I got it. Make the call," I tell him as he pulls out his phone to do just that.

My phone starts buzzing. When I pull it out of my pocket, I see King's name across the screen.

I hold up my hand for Zeke to hold off, then I press accept on the call.

"WHAT THE FUCK DID YOU DO?" King's voice comes booming across the line. "You've gone too far this time, Gabe. This can't be undone. The Castros will be coming after both of us."

"Maybe you should have thought about all of that before you set this train into motion. And stop calling me Gabe. You sound like an idiot. We aren't friends, King. You lost that title a long time ago. Just because I've held off from putting a bullet between your eyes does not mean that I've suddenly changed my mind about it. You'll get what's coming to you. But first, I'll take pride in watching everything around you burn to ash."

I hang up the phone before he has the chance to say anything else. Honestly, I just wanted to hear his reaction since I couldn't be there to see his face.

Cain parks his bike on the side of the building beside the dumpster and covers it with a tarp. He hops into a beat-up old pickup truck and pulls up beside me.

"You boys ready?" Cain says, with a shit-eating grin on his face.

"Hell yeah! Make the call, Zeke. Let's get this show on the road," I command as the three of us take off. Zeke heads north out of town, while I follow Cain on my bike. He wanted to do this mission on his own, but I can't take that risk.

Chapter Seventeen

ANGEL

Dante left in a hurry when he received the phone call from Zeke, leaving me alone with all these toxic thoughts. Thoughts I should not be having. I tried to hide the sadness in my expression when D said his father was shot, but the look on his face was a dead giveaway that he could see the concern in my eyes. Even if he didn't mention it before he ran out the door.

When did I start giving a shit about what happens to Gabriel?

After everything he's done to the people in this town, I shouldn't give a damn. Hell, after everything he's done to me. He deserves whatever fate is coming to him. Why would I care if he's shot and probably bleeding out on his deathbed right now?

He's the enemy. Always has been. Always will be. I. Do. Not. Care that he's hurt.

Fuck, I wish that I could stop caring that he's hurt.

This internal battle is becoming a real fuckin' problem. I know I shouldn't, but I just can't help myself. The anxiety over what is going to happen to Gabe is taking over me, and I think I'm even more messed up in the head than I realized.

It feels like a ton of bricks sitting on my chest. My breaths are coming quickly as the panic settles deep inside me. He showed me a side of him that I'm sure not many people have ever seen. Including Dante.

I pace back and forth across the room, looking at my keys out of the corner of my eye. They are sitting on the coffee table. I could easily grab them and head over to the Sons of Diablo clubhouse, or the hospital... Shit, I don't even know where he is. I sure as hell can't ask Dante for that piece of information.

Fuck, I have to stay put and wait to hear something from someone...anyone. Since no one on this fucking planet has any idea that I give two shits about Gabriel, I'm sure that call will never come in.

I try to force a few deep breaths to calm down. He'll make it through this and be back to stalking my life in no time. He's a fighter. A survivor.

He still has havoc to wreak in this god-forsaken town.

My phone rings and I rush over to the counter to answer it. It's Jax...

"Hello," I answer.

"Angel, are you still at the house?" Jax says, sounding out of breath.

"Where else would I be in the middle of the night? It's not like I'm in a motorcycle club that calls me to come running at all hours." The venom in my voice comes out harsher than I want. Jax doesn't deserve that. "I'm sorry. It's just—" I stop myself before saying too much. "Yeah, Jax, I'm at home."

"What the hell was that about? You know what, never mind. Is Dante still with you? He's not answering his phone," he asks.

"No, he left a few minutes after you did. Why?" I have a feeling I know why, but I need to hear it for myself.

"Because his psycho-ass daddy just blew up the Reapers' warehouses and just caused a shit storm to come raining down on us. King's on a warpath. Not that I give a fuck, except whatever he plans to do next is not gonna be pretty. I need to make sure D is far away from the Sons right now," Jax explains.

"Well, I don't know where he is, but I'm pretty sure he's on his way to see Gabe. You know, since he was just shot. It was probably King's sorry-ass too. I wouldn't put it past him. Like he hasn't done enough to Gabe." I drift off in thought, not being able to finish what I was saying. The image of King shooting Gabe plays in mind.

"What the fuck, Trouble? You actually care about him, don't you? Oh my God. I can't believe this shit. What the fuck are you thinking? How did this happen? I thought I was damaged, but fuck... Did we really break you that bad when we left? It must have been pretty bad if you turned to fuckin' Gabriel. What? The spoiled-ass Princess couldn't have all of her men chasing her around all the time so she threw them all away and turned to the mother fucking devil. I can't even believe you."

Wow. That actually stung a little, but you know what? Fuck it. They don't get to judge me. No one does. I burst into laughter. "So you really think a lot of yourself, don't you? You might have broken me a little. Hell, I'll give you that, Jaxon. As for me caring about Gabriel? Well, that's none of your damn business. Maybe he understands me a hell of a lot more than you do. Spoiled Princess, huh? Why don't you tell me how you really feel? No. Better yet. Just keep that shit to yourself. I don't need this shit from you or anyone else." I hang the phone up and turn it on silent.

I don't need this.

Fuck him and anyone else who has something to say about me or how I live my life. The only people that I answer to are God and my mama. Last time I checked, he was neither. I'm a grown-ass woman and I'll do what I want, when I want, and how I want.

I don't give a damn what anyone thinks about it. They don't have to live my life or be in it for that matter.

Who said I have feelings for Gabriel, anyway? Just because I'm concerned for his well-being doesn't mean I have feelings for the man.

I'm over this shit. My life has gone from bad to worse in the span of two weeks. I just need sleep and hopefully I'll have calmed down by the time morning rolls around.

Maybe Dante will have an update about Gabe for me by then.

I flip off the lights in the living room and head into my bedroom. As soon as I get settled in and comfortable, I hear a noise coming from the direction of the back door. I get up slowly, trying not to make a sound. I grab my phone from the nightstand and take my switchblade out of the drawer.

I send Lucky a quick text telling him that I think someone's trying to get in my house and set the phone back down. I move around to hide behind the bedroom door, hoping to catch my intruder off guard. The door handle turns at a slow speed, as if they are being careful to not make a noise.

Thankfully, I wasn't asleep yet, or this could have been a completely different situation. I may be small, but the self-defense classes that Cassie and I went to are starting to pay off.

I steady my breathing, waiting for them to enter the room. The door opens and they move forward, almost in reach. Just one more step and I can make my move.

The tall and bulky shadow turns to look behind them, then back at the bed. They take a few steps forward to get a better look.

Bingo, motherfucker!

I move quickly. Aiming my blade for his neck, hoping for maximum damage, but it lands just below my target area. I pull the knife out as he yells in pain. I don't recognize his voice, but I have to stay focused. Never underestimate your enemy. I go to stab at him again and he grabs my wrist. I quickly drop the blade, catching it with my other hand, stabbing him in the side. I feel his blood on my hands as I retract the knife and swing it again. This time slicing his side. His grip on my wrist tightens, and he uses his size to his advantage, twisting me around and pulling my back to his chest.

He wraps my other arm around my body. Holding it in place and making me drop my knife to the ground below us.

"Fuck, you're a feisty one, aren't you?" my attacker growls into my ear. Chills shoot up my spine at the sound of his voice.

It suddenly hits me. This is the same fucker who shot up Sunnyside.

Oh hell, no.

I don't know what he wants with me, but I'm not going down without a fight.

I take a deep breath, thinking over everything that I learned in class. Exhaling, I relax my body and drop to the ground. This fucker wasn't prepared for that move. I don't waste a second of time. I turn and punch him in the balls with all my might.

Scrambling to my feet, I grab my blade off the floor and stab him one last time, leaving it embedded in his body. Turning, I take off, heading for the back door. Hopefully, this dipshit left it open or unlocked so that I can make my escape.

Running as fast as I can through the house, I hit the back door. I can hear him following behind me, but he's moving slowly. I swing the door wide open and come barreling out. I'm stopped in my tracks at the sight in front of me.

"Cass, what the hell are you doing here?" I yell out to her.

"Lucky sent me to check on you. He couldn't get here right away. Then...well...this happened," she responds, wiggling in her captor's arms.

"Shit. I'm so sorry, Cass."

"What? No warm welcome for me, sweetheart?" Gabriel chuckles.

"Fuck off. Aren't you supposed to be dead or something? Weasley bastard," I snap back.

The other dickwad then decides to make an appearance. Coming over to us while bleeding all over my yard. Great, Mom is going to have a cow when she sees this.

Gabe bursts into a fit of laughter. "You let my sweetheart get the best of you, Cain." He pulls a zip tie out of his back pocket and binds Cassie's hands together, then drags her across the yard. When he hands a zip tie to Cain, I back up and look around for something to help get us out of this mess.

Cain grabs my wrist and my instincts take over. I take a swing at him, which he quickly dodges and snatches my other wrist.

Gabe pulls out a gun and aims it at Cassie's temple. "No more fighting, sweetheart. I'd hate for my finger to slip and splatter your friend's pretty little brain all over the yard. Think of what your mother would say. And Lucky. You wouldn't want him to come home and see his sister's body out here just because you couldn't behave, now would you?"

The fight leaves my body, and I hold out my wrists for Cain. "What happened to the guy that poured his soul out on my bathroom floor not even twelve hours ago? Or was that all an act too?" My body is shaking from the adrenaline. I can't help the tears that fall from my eyes.

I'm so angry. Angry that I fell for his bull-shit. That I was actually concerned whether he would live or die.

"Let's go. Walk," Cain says, pushing me forward. We make our way out of the backyard to a beat-up truck parked in the driveway. Cain pulls down the tailgate and lifts me up, placing me in the back, then does the same to Cass.

"Is this your master plan? I'm not above jumping out of moving vehicles," I spit at the two of them.

"I have no doubt about that," Gabe says, taking out a vile of liquid from his jacket and dabbing some onto his bandana. I shuffle to the back of the truck bed as Gabe hops in the back with us.

He places the bandana over Cassie's nose and mouth. She struggles for a few seconds before she passes out.

He moves over to me, doing the same as he did with Cass. He leans down and whispers in my ear, "I'm sorry, sweetheart. You deserve better than this."

I try shaking my head to tell him no. He's not sorry for any of this. How could he be? I can't get my muscles to work and my eyes are feeling heavy. I look up at him as he lays my body down in the back of the truck. His face is the last thing I see before everything fades to black...

Chapter Eighteen

DANTE

Parking my bike in front of the Sons of Diablo's clubhouse, I look around at the empty parking lot. I get a weird vibe but decide to check inside. It's empty. Not a soul in sight. "Hellooo," I yell into the abandoned void of space. Nothing but the echo of my own voice reaches my ears.

I pull out my phone, checking to see if I have any missed calls. Nothing. Maybe Gabriel was worse off than Zeke thought, and he decided to take him to the hospital instead. I dial Zeke's number and the voicemail immediately filters through the speaker. So I try Gabriel's phone and it just rings until his voicemail answers. I call a few of the other guys, but no one is picking up.

I'm his fucking son. If something has happened to him, I better be the first to know. "Fuck!" I scream into the abyss of the clubhouse.

Where the hell is everyone?

Grabbing a handful of my hair, I tug it in frustration. Nothing comes to mind about who else to call or what to do next.

I walk outside the clubhouse ready to go check the hospitals to see if I can find my dad. He has to be somewhere. As soon as I hit the door, I hear the rumble of motorcycles coming up the road.

Thank God! How did I beat them here?

Two bikes pull around the corner. The first thing I notice is these guys aren't Sons, but the Reapers of Havoc instead. A total of ten motorcycles pull in, parking beside me.

Nerves about tonight's events and years of training have me pulling out the gun that's tucked in the back of my pants. It may not be much, but if I go down then I'll at least take a few of these fuckers out with me.

Lucky jumps off his bike and runs my way. He places himself between me and the Reapers as a human barrier. Royal and Jaxon make their way over to me, following suit. "What the fuck is going on here?" I ask, hoping someone gives me some information soon because my head is spinning.

Lucky turns toward me. "Where's your dad, D? I know you don't want any part of this shit. Just tell us where he is and we'll go."

"The hell we will. Who died and left you in charge, boy?" This comes from one of the older Reapers as he makes his way from the back of the pack to the front to stare us down. He pushes people out of his way and doesn't stop until the only thing separating us are Royal's and Jaxon's bodies. That's still not close enough for him, so he leans his head between theirs and over their shoulders.

Getting within an inch of my face, he threatens, "You'll tell us where he is or I'll put a bullet in that pretty boy head of yours."

Royal steps forward, shoving the guy back to put some space between us. "Not gonna happen, sicko. Just chill the fuck out for a minute." Royal turns, taking my arm and leading me away from the rest of the group. "Just tell me where he's at, D. Is he here? These guys are ready to tear this place apart, and I don't want you in the middle of it," he explains.

"He's not here. I have no clue where he is."

"So why is this place empty? Did they move out and forget to tell you or what? I'm going to be real with you. This shit is looking really suspicious, D."

"You want me to make some shit up? Because I don't know what to tell you. I got a call saying Gabriel was shot and to meet them here. I show up and it's a damn ghost town. I've called everyone. No one is picking up their phone. So that's it. That's all I know. Now take these fuckers and go," I say, pointing to the guys lined up behind him who are ready for war.

Lucky walks over and claps me on the shoulder. "Sorry about this, D. Your dad did some fucked-up shit, brother. The boys just wanna find him and deal with it before we get our asses handed to us by the cartel."

"I get it, Luck, but I can't tell you what I don't know. I may have my own issues with Gabriel, but that doesn't mean I'm just going to hand him over to the Reapers so you guys can take your anger out on him. Especially since I don't know what is going on," I respond back.

Lucky nods his head because he gets it. I may be a part of the Sons in name, but nothing else. My club doesn't trust me. Only the younger members really talk to me. I'm only asked to do low-level jobs by those higher up in rank.

Whatever this shit's about, they failed to clue me in on it.

"Where's King, anyway? Why isn't *he* here ready to wreak havoc on us?" I ask Royal.

"He took off to look for your dad and Cruz went after him, but he's losing it. After the shit that happened with Angel, and now this? I think it's just pushed him past the point of no return. I don't know what's gotten into him, but he's fuckin' gone, man."

Royal looks over at the Reapers waiting on him. "I need to get them out of here."

Lucky's phone starts to ring as he and Royal walk back toward the others. Taking a quick glance at the screen, he puts it to his ear before I hear, "What the fuck do you mean she's gone? Mom, just hang on. I'm on my way." Lucky ends the call and runs over to his bike with Royal and me following behind him.

"What's going on, Luck?" I ask him.

"Cass and Angel are both missing. My mom's flipping her shit. Brenda's on her way home from work. This isn't good, guys. It takes a lot for my mom to freak out the way she is. This is Gabriel, right? More of his fucked-up mind games to get back at us. Fuck! I gotta get over there," he says, trying to bury the worry in his voice, but I hear it loud and clear.

"You both better pray they turn up unharmed. Otherwise, I'm going to burn this gotdamn town to the ground." He starts up his bike and takes off. I know how much the women in his life mean to him. He'll stop at nothing to protect them.

Royal turns to the Reapers, yelling out to them, "Let's ride, boys." He turns to me and asks, "You coming, brother?"

I nod in return, and we take off with the rest of the Reapers in tow. Speeding over to Angel's and Lucky's houses.

Darkness fades into an early morning dawn as the sun begins to rise higher into the sky. I've only had a few hours of rest. It wasn't long after I fell asleep that Jax and Angel woke me with their debauchery. Not that I'm complaining. I'd prefer to be awakened like that every day of my life if it means I get to spend my nights next to Angel.

Unfortunately, the drama never rests in this town. Apparently, neither do my father's diabolical schemes to destroy King and the Reapers. I know his hate for King runs deep, but whenever I try to ask why, he just shuts down and barricades his secrets within his mind.

I've tried for years to find out the backstory there. It's like he just doesn't want me to know. There was a time when I was growing up that I looked up to my father. I remember thinking he was some kind of superhero, but all that seems so long ago. The memories are like broken pieces of a shattered vase that I can't quite put back together.

Thinking back, I can't pinpoint the exact moment that he changed. Maybe it happened over time. Those years after my mom passed away are such a blur. It's like he went from being super-dad to nothing with the snap of a finger. Sometimes I wonder if any of the memories I have of him from that time are real or if they are just a figment of my imagination. Maybe it was just my mind playing tricks on me and giving me visions of the dad I wish he would've been.

Now it may be too late to repair all the damage that's been done between the two of us. I still have no clue if he's even really hurt or if it's all a part of his elaborate plans. It's pretty sad that I can't even trust the words of the man who's telling me that my dad has been shot and could be dying.

With the Sons ignoring my calls, I can't do much about my father until I can find him and see for myself what condition he's in. But I can help Lucky figure out what's going on with the girls, so that's what I'll focus my attention on for now.

We pull up to the house at the same time that Brenda's car pulls into the driveway. She hops out of the driver's seat and runs toward the house. She doesn't even bother to close the car door behind her.

Royal and I chase after her, cutting her off at the front door. I wrap my arms around her, lifting her off the ground just before she's able to enter the house. Royal stands in the doorway of the front entrance, blocking her path.

"Brenda, please let one of us go in before you. We don't know what we are walking into here," Royal pleads with her.

"No. Put me down. I need to see it for myself. This is my house, and it's my daughter who's missing. Let me go, Dante. Now," Brenda yells. I reluctantly place her feet back on the ground.

She stalks toward the door. With her hand held over the knob, she pauses for a brief second to take in a deep breath, and then she opens it up wide enough for us to follow after her. We walk into the front room where Lucky is sitting on the couch consoling his mother, Ashley. His eyes meet mine with a dark sadness in them, and he shakes his head. "No, Brenda. Don't go back there. You don't need to see this," he warns, and Brenda chokes out a sob when she notices the red stains on her champagne-colored carpet. The blood is coming from the hallway and leads to the back door.

I grab her hand, giving it a little squeeze for some sort of comfort. Even though I'm completely terrified at what we are about to see, I try to be strong for her.

We follow the trail of blood that leads to Angel's room. My heart drops to the pit of my stomach as we take in the messy sight before us. There's a large amount of dried, dark red blood in one spot that's seeped deep into the carpet. There's more on the door frame in what looks like a man's bloody handprint. Angel's switchblade is laying on the ground stained with her victory.

"This is too big to be Angel's hand. It has to be the attackers. That's good, right? It means that our girl fought back. Whoever came after her is hurt," Royal concludes.

"My baby's a fighter. She always has been. She didn't go down quietly," Brenda sobs as I wrap her in my arms, trying to bring her any semblance of comfort. It's what Angel would want, and she'd expect nothing less from us.

She pulls out of my embrace. "Thank you, Dante. Thank you both. Angel is so lucky to have you in her life. We all are." She looks between Royal and me, giving us a crooked, half broken smile.

Brenda turns back to me, taking my chin in her fingers, forcing me to look down into her gaze. "Your mother must have been a saint because there's no way that bastard's blood runs through your veins. You are too good and he's too...evil to have raised a son with a heart like yours. One made of pure gold." She looks away, breaking our eye contact. "I'm sorry. I know that he's your father, but he's gone too far this time. He's terrorized this town, and everyone in it turns a blind eye. Even the police. He literally gets away with murder. Now, he's taken two beautiful, innocent girls who deserve nothing but the world. He deserves a fate worse than death."

She pats my arm and walks out of the room before I have a chance to respond. Not that I know how to respond to that. I mean, what do I say? Deep down, I know she's right. But for some reason, I keep holding onto hope that my gut feeling is wrong, that maybe this is all a big mistake and my dad doesn't have a heavy hand in all of this.

But the reality sits deep within my mind. I mean, he's missing, so are Angel and Cassie. Plus, no one is answering their phones. Not to mention his new obsession with her, needing to stalk and know her whereabouts at all times. It's all just too much of a coincidence.

"Snap out of it, brother. Let's see what we can figure out," Royal says, snapping me out of the pity party that I'm quickly drowning in. He takes me by the arm and drags me out of the room.

Royal and I follow the blood trail, making our way to the backyard and then back around to the driveway where the trail ends.

"They were parked here," he concludes. Pointing to the corner of the neighbor's house, he says, "So if one of the neighbors' security cameras picked up the vehicle's license plate, that will give us a lead or at least a place to start." I look up at Royal, fear filling his features. "We'll find them. All of them. Can you get some of the guys to start going door to door, asking the neighbors if we can look at their surveillance footage?"

"I'm on it," he agrees, running over to the Reapers, who have been patiently waiting to find out what's going on.

I watch a few of them split off to the houses surrounding us. Out of my peripheral, I see two of them hurrying to get inside Angel's house.

"The boys are going to head up the north side of the street. You and I will go south. Let's see what we can find out."

I deflate a little under the crushing weight of my worry for Angel, wishing we didn't have to do this. "C'mon man, our girl needs saving." Royal's words are filled with sorrow and determination.

Hang on a little longer, Heaven. We're coming for you. We can't live this life without you.

First and foremost, I'd like to thank my family for loving me and supporting this crazy dream of mine. Brook, Kam, A, and Sissy, you have pushed me to be a better person, writer and mother. There were so many times I wanted to give up and you pushed me to keep going. I love you more than you will ever understand.

My Alpha and Beta teams, you ladies are such a blessing. I'm so thankful to have you by my side through this journey.

My ARC and Street teams, you all are the MVPs promoting my books all over social media.

To my readers, thank you for taking a chance on a new baby author and loving the story and these characters that have been stuck in my head for so long now.